MURDER
AT
MALAFORTUNA

By
J. Tracksler

Llumina Press

Copyright 2003 J. Tracksler

All rights reserved. No part of this publication may be reproduced or transmitted in any form or by any means electronic or mechanical, including photocopy, recording, or any information storage and retrieval system, without permission in writing from both the copyright owner and the publisher.

Requests for permission to make copies of any part of this work should be mailed to Permissions Department, Llumina Press, PO Box 772246, Coral Springs, FL 33077-2246

ISBN: 193230374X
Printed in the United States of America

DEDICATED

To the memory of Dora Forte Hastings.
You are missed, *bella amica mia.*

And also to the real Moe and Blanche,
and to Chauncy D'Elia's classic store,
the inspiration for Fancy's.

cover design by bryce creative, kittery point, maine

CHAPTER ONE

If it hadn't been for Claudio Boccadoro's abscessed tooth, there wouldn't have been two murders. Claudio would have delivered the letter to his neighbor by his own hand attached by his shoulder and chin to his wagging mouth. Completely at ease in nosing around in everyone on his route's private business, Claudio would have noted the foreign address on the envelope immediately. Everyone knew that Claudio couldn't keep a thing to himself, so the news that one of the villagers had received a letter from America would have been passed from doorstep to doorstep as fast as Claudio's bicycle could pedal, taking time out, naturally, for a cup of tea or a snack that was offered along the way. The neighbors would have speculated endlessly, sparked by Claudio's insatiable curiosity about everything that went on in the village. The woman at the green house would have discussed it with her neighbor in the yellow house. And from there, the gossip would have spread to the people who lived in the house with the wisteria tree next door. Who would be writing a letter from America? . . . And why, for goodness sake? . . . Every possible scenario would have been discussed . . . America! Imagine! What *could* be in the envelope?

But Claudio's tooth woke him in the middle of the night with a pain that made him howl. His wife jumped out of bed and made him a poultice of cornmeal and hot water and gave him two of the little white pills left over from the time she slipped and sprained her ankle. Claudio never managed to get back to sleep and his wife, as weary as he was, called the *dentista* early in the morning and made an emergency appointment for ten o'clock that very morning. She then called Claudio's boss at *L'ufficio Postale* to tell him that Claudio wouldn't be able to deliver the mail that morning.

Claudio's boss thought about the time two years ago when he had to have his own molar torn from his mouth. He clutched his hand to his cheek and closed his eyes, remembering how much the damn thing had hurt. Poor Claudio would probably be out for a few days. Maybe more. He'd better get Benno Catale over here from Lanzio to deliver the mail in Malafortuna for the entire next week, just to be sure.

And so the letter from America was delivered to Malafortuna by a complete stranger, someone who had no interest whatsoever in the business of the inhabitants of the sleepy little town. Someone who didn't care at *all* that a letter had arrived from America for one of their own. No, Benno Catale, the *postino* from another town, was a man who was dependable and efficient with no curiosity or imagination. He simply slapped the letter, which would lead to the brutal murder of two innocent people, together with two bills and a highly colored flyer from the local *fruttivendolo* into the basket outside the front door of *Numero Quattro Strada della Chiesa* and then continued to the next house; unaware of the beginning part he had played in the upcoming tragedy.

CHAPTER TWO

Julie opened the menu and her worst fears were confirmed. *Pine*apple ravioli! Pineapple Ravioli napped with a blueberry-lime coulis with a confit of gingered mango. *Jesus on a toothpick*! She mentally gagged and then took a ladylike sip of water to try and control herself.

He peered at her from over the top of his menu. "Mmmmmm, everything looks so good, doesn't it?" She nodded, unable to speak, stunned anew by the Chinese Blowfish with Broccoli Rabe. Napped with Raspberry Sauce. Napped! Napped! Every freaking thing was *napped*! The only thing that should be napped--ever--was a baby's bottom.

She really hadn't wanted to go out tonight. Mariah had forced her. "You haven't had a date in two months, Julie. A Class A woman like yourself, you gotta get into circulation again." Just to keep Mariah quiet, she'd sighed yes and three days later Mariah announced that it was all fixed up. A new friend of Brucie's, his name was Roger Arkwright. Originally from California, a real catch. A super successful financier on Wall Street. Tall. Personable. What more could Julie possibly want?

"What did you tell him about me?"

"That you were gorgeous, a redhead, grey eyes that show the depths of your soul, tall," Mariah sketched a wiggle in the air, "A talented chef sought by every restaurant company in New York." Mariah's big blue eyes were huge with innocence.

"And what else?" Julie's expression was skeptical.

"That you'd been through a bummer of a divorce recently and wanted to meet some new people." The blue eyes brimmed with sincerity. Julie's heart sank. It would be awful.

Mariah answered the door, almost gushing when she brought him in. He brought flowers and looked, well, OK, even though Julie wasn't crazy about the thin blonde mustache that sat on his upper lip. *Looks like a caterpillar*, she thought and then she chastised herself. *Come on, give the guy a chance. He's really kind of good looking.*

"I thought we'd try that trendy new restaurant on 55th," he said, "The one called The Hills of Tuscany. Brucie told me you were into Italian foods." Mentally, she slapped herself in the head. She *hated* trendy restaurants, especially pseudo-Italian ones that stuck "Tuscan" into their names. Tuscan this, Tuscan that. Overused and generally disappointing. It was a big joke at culinary school, just name your restaurant The Tuscan Something, and great hoards of fools, trying desperately to be fashionable, will rush to your door. She sighed. She'd promised Mariah she would try. She smiled at Roger and told him that it sounded wonderful. Over his shoulder, she could see Mariah nodding, making encouraging faces and giving her a thumb's up sign. She gave Mariah a sour look and picked up her coat.

The in-people crowds were certainly circling around the bronzed doorway of The Hills of Tuscany. Dozens of people lined up, nearly around the block. Acting as if he owned the street, Roger shouldered his way through the riff-raff and clasped the hand of the employee manning the door. *It must have been a fifty-dollar bill*, Julie thought, as the man snapped an immediate oily smile at Roger. The golden rope parted and the door to Tuscan delights was opened to them.

Roger immediately grabbed the hand of the *maitre d'* and Julie strained her eyes to see what denomination made him bow so obsequiously low. They were led to a table in an alcove and a snap of the fingers summoned their waiter. Roger's face had that smug look men tended to wear when they felt they had pulled off a coup. Julie admonished herself severely for her thoughts. The guy was just trying to show her a nice time, that's all. She smiled brightly across the table and Roger's eyes took on a shine. She'd be a good little girl and play the part of the date who was stunned by her escort's savior faire.

"Hi! I'm Chandler and I'll be your server tonight!" Chandler smiled mechanically at them and gave them a little wave. "I'll be right back," he caroled as he plunked two menus on the table and disappeared before Roger could even open his mouth.

Roger shrugged. "It's murder to even get into here," he confided in a solemn whisper. "They're *so* selective." Julie smiled again and opened her menu. She was amused to see that hers had no prices on it. So trendy. She scanned the appetizers and groaned inwardly. God save us all! Pistachio Polenta with Raspberry-Thyme Cream and Roasted Garlic. Penne with Buttermilk and Fire Roasted Duck Rillettes. She folded the menu and put it back on the table. Roger was still hidden behind his. "Everything looks so good!" he enthused. She made some sound of agreement and looked around, noting the sleek self-satisfied elegance of the diners and the expensive furnishings replicating someone's idea of a Tuscan grotto. After two years at The New York Culinary School, she recognized all the signs of a very successful eatery, one that catered to every whim of the urban *cognoscati's* ever-changing insatiable need to be different. One making money hand over fist.

Roger placed his menu down with a sigh of contentment. "Now," he leaned forward, "tell me about yourself, Julie." She opened her mouth . . . "I work with Brucie's account at Grovener and Garth," he continued. "I snagged the firm away from George Atwell the first week I was here in The Big Apple." Julie winced slightly and closed her mouth, biting at her bottom lip. "They were certainly happy they brought me in, let me tell you. I was Salesman of the Month the first month I was here, and, well," he managed to look smug and bashful at the same time, "I've been winning accolades ever since. It's a tough world out there, Julie, and a man has to reach for what he wants." Roger looked around for the waiter and snapped his fingers trying to get his attention. "Fortunately, I've been able to not only reach for it, Julie, but I've also, heh, heh, grabbed it and made it mine." His handsome vacant face reflected his pride. "Now, let's hear more about you, my dear." Julie opened her mouth again . . . .

"So sorry, sir," the waiter appeared like a wraith. "We're terribly, terribly busy tonight and," he bent over cozily and confided, "that's Michael Douglas' agent at the table in the corner." Roger craned his neck to see, and the waiter smirked. "Now, what would you like to drink, sir? We have a lovely Merlot tonight. *Faaa*bulous. Cranford Woods Reserve '85. Scored a 97 in Wine Spectator." Roger looked suitably impressed and nodded in a way to let Julie know that he understood the Ways of Great Wine. Then he conferred with Chandler, his manner intense, man to man, showing Julie again that he was one with the deep masculine secrets of the correct selection of vintage wines. Julie sat back and wondered how she'd get through the night.

She hadn't always been like this, had she? Wasn't there a time when all of this stuff would have impressed her? Well, maybe way back, before she married Stephen. Before the divorce. Before culinary school had opened her eyes to the rape of food in the name of profit. Before her bruised soul had tired of pretense and falseness. She was sure she'd been a much nicer person back then.

She answered the waiter's question. "The Merlot? No, thank you. I'll just have a glass of house wine. Red, please." Roger and Chandler looked mutually affronted. Roger ordered the Merlot for himself and he and Chandler shared a smirky sort of smile which managed to sneer at Julie's choice and approve of Roger's at the same time.

"You'll love the Merlot. It's *faaa*bulous," Chandler caroled as he wafted away once more.

Roger gave Julie his best intense look. "Now, let's get back to you. For starters, are you originally from New York?"

Julie waited a moment and when Roger didn't begin talking about himself answered, "No. I've lived here for two years while I went to school. I 'm from Greenwich, Connecticut."

Roger's eyes widened in appreciation. "Greenwich! That's where all the big corporate offices are! Isn't it one of the most expensive towns in America?" She shrugged and he eyed her with predatory new interest. "And don't a lot of movie stars and millionaires live there?" She nodded and was fascinated to note that the tip of his tongue actually came out and licked his upper lip. "And, um, does your family, um, live there?" His eyes glittered and he leaned forward over the table.

"Well, yes. My mother and father and most of my family still live there." He was entranced. She waved her hands in the air dismissively, "We've been there for ages, it's not a big deal . . ." she tried to explain, but he cut her off.

"Greenwich!" If possible, he leaned even further over the table, locking his eyes to hers. "Does your family own property there?" He sucked in his breath, reverent, and waited for her answer.

She sat back. What the hell. She'd make him a happy man. "Yes. We've been in Greenwich for generations. My family has owned a business there since the turn of the century." Roger's eyes were gleaming. "It's where I grew up. I married a Greenwich man and we lived there for the two years we were married." She hoped she was giving him a bit of rope.

She was. "Do you still own a house there?"

"No. The house and the marriage disappeared."

He looked a bit crestfallen, but then rose back gamely. "Oh, dear. I hope you got a big settlement," he probed delicately. She shrugged girlishly, managing to convey a lot of meaning. "What happened? To your marriage,

I mean?" She knew, simply knew, that he wanted to ask what happened to the settlement but just couldn't figure out quite how to do it.

"Just didn't work out." She would never tell him one blessed thing about it. About the heartbreak and deceit. About her innocence and stupidity. About how Stephen had cheated on her from the very day that they'd wed.

He persisted. "So does your family have a big house in Greenwich? I hear lots of media people live there. Television stars and the really rich." His face was avid and he was almost babbling. She nodded, dangling her hook. "And there are some really wonderful places, country estates and mansions on the water." She must have made some kind of sound because he sucked in his breath. "Do you live in one of those places?" She nodded again. It was true. Sort of true anyway. The Sabatinos *did* live in a couple of big houses. Big shabby old houses. And a couple of them, including her mother and father's *were* located on Long Island Sound. Not in the ritzy section of town though. And they *did* own a big old business, but she didn't think it was quite what Roger was imagining. "Oh, I'd love to visit out there," he almost gushed. "One of the directors of our company lives nearby in Port Chester," she nodded once again. "But that's not quite as nice as Greenwich, is it?" She shrugged once more. *I don't even have to say much*, she thought to herself. *Just nod and shrug in the right places. If my head doesn't fall off before dinner, the evening might even be called a success.*

The waiter came with their wine, hers in a glass and the Merlot in a white napkin-wrapped bundle, looking much like a first-born son being presented to the family. Chandler plunked her glass of wine down in front of her and then began the tedious procedure that accompanies the purchase of a bottle of wine that costs more than ten bucks. Roger was a willing participant in the ceremony. Julie sipped at her glass of red while the two of them tried to impress one another. One of the first things she'd learned in Wine Class 101 was about house wines. Any restaurant worth it's waiting line would always have a good house wine. She held her glass by the stem and inhaled. Not too shabby.

Chandler stood back reverently, his hands clasped together, while Roger held up his glass, admiring the color. He swirled the wine around just the way it told you how to in the better men's magazines. A bubble of laughter surged as Julie thought about Uncle Romeo who made his wine by the barrel every year and drank it out of a jug thrown over his shoulder. Uncle Romeo would howl at all this theatrical nonsense. Roger took her chuckle to be one of admiration and launched into lengthy psycho-babble about the art of wine tasting. He and Chandler nearly embraced one another in their mutual congratulations over the beauty of the Merlot. With one final satisfied smirk, the waiter finally withdrew. Roger sipped at his Merlot and his face was set in the proper reverence for a bottle of wine that was going to cost him over three hundred dollars.

"Do you want to try some of this?" he asked. "It's *faaa*bulous."

"No." She shook her head again and her hair flew out in a coppery sheen. "The house wine is very good." She smiled at him. She'd try. She'd really try. "Tell me about yourself, Roger." And he did. He talked for forty-five minutes, raving about himself, his education, his work, his successes and his ruthlessness in business. He told her about the deals he'd made, laughing about the competition that he'd crushed along the way. He told her about his ambitions. To be at the top. To marry well. To have everything. As he talked and talked, she began to look around for their waiter. She was starved. Entranced by his own story, Roger droned on and on. Every third word was "I" and everything said was said to impress her. In hungry desperation, she interrupted a detailed explanation of Roger's latest coup by opening her menu and glancing at it.

"Oh, er . . . " Roger's monolog slowed down. "Perhaps we should order." He opened his own menu. "I hear the food here is *faaa*bulous." He glanced at the menu for a moment and then told her in a conspiratorial voice, "Don't worry about the prices. Have anything you want." She grinned and assured him that she would. He laughed, including her in his conspiracy, "I mean really, go ahead, order the most expensive thing. This is all covered by my expense account," he confided. "To the boss, you're an important client so I don't have to pay for anything myself. The sky's the limit, Julie."

So he's a cheat on top of everything else, she sighed to herself. *Please God, let me get through this night quickly.* She nodded one more time and put her menu down.

Roger looked around and saw Chandler at the serving station, talking with one of the other waiters. He snapped his fingers. Chandler continued to talk, nudging his fellow worker in the ribs and laughing out loud. Roger called, "Oh, waiter!" Then, a little louder, "Chandler! Over here!"

Chandler turned and glared for a moment, flapping his hand to indicate that he'd be along. Roger looked at his menu again. "I'm having the Pink Grapefruit Lasagne Napped with Bourbon Sauce. It's the Chef's Signature Dish," he gave the words capital letters. "How about you?"

Julie's stomach lurched at the thought of Pink Grapefruit Lasagne. "I haven't quite made up my mind."

Chandler glided to their table. "So sorry about that. Have you decided yet?" He looked at Roger. "I recommend the Boeuf Verdi." He pronounced it *boof* and waved his hands in the air for emphasis. Roger gave his suggestion grave thought. "It's *faaa*bulous," urged Chandler. He and Roger discussed at some length the merits of the *boof* versus the lasagne. Roger finally selected the lasagne to Chandler's approval and then added a salad of baby field greens with jicama and passion fruit with a warm lime and ginger dressing. Chandler rubbed his hands together and turned to Julie.

"And Madam?"

"I'll have *linguini aglio e olio* and a steak, very, very rare," she said to him. "Please tell the chef I'd like it 'Pittsburgh'."

He stared at her. "What?" he said, in a flat, Brooklyn tone. She repeated her order, giving the words her best flagrant accent. "It's not on the menu," he told her with a mean triumphant little smile.

"I know." She grinned back, one food service person to another. "Please write it down like this: *Linguini al dente* with garlic and olive oil and a steak, bloody rare. They'll know in the kitchen". Her smile became kindly and he almost sneered at her. He dubiously glanced at Roger for confirmation and the two of them shrugged their shoulders at the same time. Chandler turned abruptly and walked away, clearly in a huff.

"Julie," Roger chided her gently, "There's no need to upset him. They're so sensitive here," he shook his head gently from side to side and waggled his finger. "Try not to hurt his feelings, my dear." She sat back with her pretty mouth open slightly. He patted her hand. "You said some Italian words, didn't you? Do you speak Italian?"

She bit back what she almost said. "A little," she told him. "Mostly food words. My family is Italian with a little Irish thrown in."

"Ah," Roger said. "That explains it." Before she could ask what he meant, he continued, "And the red hair is the Irish part." She shrugged. It simply wasn't worth it. "I thought your last name was Stanton?"

"It is. Stanton is part of my ex-husband's legacy." She grinned inwardly at the expression on his face. "My given name is Giulietta Sabatino." She said it with as much of an accent as she possibly could.

"Oh, Sabatino." She could see his mind churning, rearranging some things. "And, uh, what does the, uh, Sabatino family do in Greenwich?" His question was delicately put.

Her answer was just as delicate. "They're in environmental matters."

"That's a very hot area," he said with pomposity, obviously relieved at her answer. "Lots of money to be made there." His voice became sententious. "And your corporate offices are in Greenwich?"

She answered eagerly, "They've been there for generations, as I said. The Sabatino Corporation is a growing concern, interacting on a daily basis with some of the largest corporations and wealthiest people in the world, and profit is, um, picking up more and more."

Roger buttered his roll, happy with the direction her answers were taking. "Lots of profit, you say?" She nodded once again. "And, do you, uh, are you, uh, part of the corporate structure?" There, he'd finally asked.

"Oh, yes." She almost gushed. "My parents are retired now, although my father still keeps his, um, hands in the business. My brother is the president - he's the active head of the company - you might say he's the driving force behind our current expansion." She looked down modestly. "And me? Well, although I'm listed on the letterhead as Vice President." He hung, spellbound, at her words, "I'm generally a silent partner, living off the leftovers, so to speak." She scolded herself: *Julie, you have* got *to stop this!* She looked up to meet his glittering avaricious eyes. He began to talk again, telling her how he'd like to meet her family. How much he'd always wanted to work for the betterment of the environment. How he'd be delighted to run her up to Greenwich one of these days and view their corporate headquarters. Julie nibbled at a breadstick and let him run on.

A buzzing noise interrupted Roger's monolog. "What's that?" Julie asked, looking around. Roger smirked and reached importantly into his jacket pocket. *Oh, no*, she groaned to herself. *Not a cell phone*! Several fellow diners were looking on, some with envy and some with hostility. She could hear high pitched squawks from the business end of the little phone and Roger turned his head slightly, muffling his voice with his hand. She gazed out over the heads of their fellow diners; nevertheless, she couldn't help hearing part of the conversation. "Later . . . No, not tonight . . . I said *not tonight*!" Roger surreptitiously watched her out of the corner of his eyes, trying to judge if she could hear. "Later, I said!" She busily buttered her breadstick and snapped it in two, crunching on a bite. "I can't talk now . . . ." His voice was whiny. "Of course. Of course I do . . . Me too." His face was flushed and he stuffed the telephone back into his jacket. "Important business," he told her. "I have to be available at all times. Excuse the interruption." She smiled yet again. Her face hurt, actually ached, especially around her mouth muscles.

The waiter arrived with Roger's salad and sniffily told her that the cook had laughed out loud at her order. She winked at him and he jumped back. Roger looked a little disapproving and had another glass of the Merlot. He began to talk again, a bit nervously, telling her about his wardrobe and then going into detail about the decoration of his apartment. She made a vow to kill Mariah.

The time ticked by. She was so hungry she was afraid that her stomach would start rumbling. Now Roger was asking her questions again. Asking about culinary school and where she was headed, jobwise. That was the word he used, "jobwise". "I hear culinary school graduates can nearly write their own ticket in New York City." He waited, as if he'd asked a question.

"Jobwise," she answered, "it's an excellent market, especially if one is a woman and especially if one has graduated at the head of one's class. And especially with my father's connections". Hell, she might as well jump in all the way. "I have several lucrative offers to manage executive kitchens." She watched him salivate. "All from large corporations in the city."

His head bobbed up and down, a smirk on his face. "And, uh, jobwise, um, uh, what would a starting salary be for an, um, executive chef?'

"Oh, it's pretty open," she gazed with candor into his eyes. "I'm really being courted and the offers are piling up. They're bidding in the quarter million dollar range now."

"*Really*!" He breathed in reverence. "I had no idea that chefs would be offered so much money!"

"Oh, yes," she told him truthfully. "It's a great field, jobwise."

✦ ✦ ✦

"It was just awful, Mariah. I'm never going to go out with *anyone* from New York again, especially someone who works in finance. He was such a jerk!"

"That bad, huh?"

"Worse. The food would have been OK except that the little turd of a waiter forgot to pick it up when it was ready. I'm sure he did it on purpose. My *linguini* was a pile of mush and the steak was ruined. The service sucked!

The waiter . . . Aghhh! I can't even talk about the waiter!" She paced around the room.

"Sit down, Jules. Put your feet up. Tell me." Mariah's voice was soothing.

"He . . . He was an imbecile," she sputtered. "We waited nearly an hour and a half for our food. While we were waiting, Roger told me how great he was seventy-five times and asked me how much money my family had thirty-two times!" Mariah rolled her eyes in sympathy. Julie jumped up again and began to stride up and down the room trying to contain her anger. "Then," she whirled and glared at Mariah, "the jackass was filling my wineglass and talking to another waiter at the same time. He was waving his fat little hands in the air, telling this guy all the biological details about his *faaa*bulous date last night!" Julie mimicked Chandler's performance and Mariah began to laugh. Julie's voice rose higher and higher, "And then the dork spilled the wine all over the front of my dress!" Mariah's hand crept up to her mouth, trying to stifle her snickers. "And somehow, it was supposed to be *my* fault. The waiter started to scream at me and stupid Yuppie Roger agreed with him!"

"Oh, no!"

Julie's eyes flashed. "The waiter started to have a hissy fit. Roger kept shushing him, patting him on the arm and telling *me* not to make a scene. He said that this was too sophisticated a place for me to fuss over a little wine. Then he told *me* to apologize to the waiter!" Mariah goggled. "And then, Chandler--that was his name--the little peckerhead--the waiter I mean, not Roger--stood there with this smug look on his face, waiting for my apology. He didn't even offer me a napkin or anything to help me mop up the mess he'd made!" Mariah snorted, trying not to laugh any more.

"But that's not all!" Julie's voice shook as she continued. "The *big* peckerhead--Roger--gave me a dirty look and started to apologize to the waiter. I thought he was going to lick his hand, for God's sake!" She brought herself up to her full height and put her finger across her top lip, as if she had a mustache, "Julie, my dear!" She mimicked Roger's voice, "Please stop making a scene! Apologize to Chandler at once!"

"So what did you do?"

Julie sat down, suddenly ladylike. She primly crossed her ankles and folded her hands together. "Oh, I was such a good girl. I apologized."

"You *did*? Doesn't sound like you, Jul."

"Mmmm Hmmmm. After all, my mother raised a polite daughter. I positively groveled at the little turd's feet while Roger looked on with smug-faced approval. Then," she showed Mariah how she did it, " I picked up the rest of my glass of wine and I dumped it on Roger's head." Mariah gaped. "*Then* I picked up the rest of the bottle of Merlot and poured it on *Chandler's* head and *then* I walked out of the restaurant and came home." She sighed and put her feet up on the sofa. A big sigh rolled out from the depths of her soul. "That's it. I'm going to be a nun. No more men in my life. *Ever!*"

"Sounds like you had a bad time." Mariah said inadequately.

"It was awful," Julie's voice was hushed. "But the most awful thing was me."

"You?"

"Me. I was just as bad. I egged him on. He was such a mercenary yuppie snob that I let him think we were rich and that we had a big business in Greenwich."

"Well, your family has a few bucks, Jules. You don't exactly starve up there. Sabatino's *is* a big business."

"Yeah, but not like I let him believe. He thinks Greenwich is like some kind of rich-peoples' heaven. He thought that Sabatino's was some big corporate concern." She started to giggle, remembering what she'd said. "I told him . . . I . . . Oh, Gawd, Mariah . . . I was soooooo bad!" Her laughter spilled out. "I told him that business was 'picking up'! I said that my brother Moe was 'the driving force' behind our expansion!"

"Picking up! Oh, no!" Mariah began to laugh with her. "The driving force! You didn't!"

"I did! I did!" Julie's laughter was nearly hysterical. "I never explained that Sabatino's picks up garbage for a living and that Moe drives the big truck on the route!" She fell over on the sofa and pounded the pillows with glee. "I said business was picking up!" Mariah's shouts of glee made her weak. She collapsed next to Julie and their hysteria lasted for several minutes. Julie wiped the tears of mirth from her face. "I've got to get out of here, Mariah," she said with quiet desperation.

"What do you mean?"

"I'm sick of all the phoniness. Sick of trendy food and men. Sick of the city. Sick of pretentious waiters and overpriced restaurants. Sick of yuppie men who only care about money. Sick of it all."

"So you had a lousy date. You'll be fine in the morning."

"No. I mean it. Tonight was the crowning glory of everything I want to get away from before I lose my mind. I hate New York and everything it stands for. I want to go where people are unsoiled. Where food is real. Where life is real. Where men aren't peacocks--jerks . . . and where I won't start to be the same way." She folded her arms across her chest and her lower lip stuck out. "I'm going away from all of this."

"But where will you go?" Mariah cried in anguish. "Where?"

"I don't know," Julie said to her. "Somewhere. Somewhere at the ends of the earth, that's where I'll go."

CHAPTER THREE

Massimo Nulla sat in the shade of his mother's grape arbor. His big feet, clad in regulation black boots, were propped on the table in front of him and his sky-blue, soulful eyes were closed. His long black lashes made a pattern on his sunburned cheeks. He wasn't exactly sleeping, just peacefully resting his eyes and the gossip of his mother and Nonna Graziella buzzed around his head blending into the noise the bumblebees were making.

"She's OK for a '*Mericana*. Nice to everyone."

"Mmmmmm?" Nonna's mouth was grudging. "Still, what's she really doing in this godforsaken place? 'Atsa what I really wanna know."

'Ah! You're suspicious of everyone!" Mamma threw her hands up in the air. "She's here to learn our way of cooking. Nothing more, nothing less." Nonna shrugged a reluctant maybe. "She's . . . Let's see . . . the great . . . or is it great-great granddaughter of what's his name . . . Salvatore Fiorile who went to America in 1900. I don't remember the family, but you should."

"I remember them. I remember everything."

"You don't remember what day it is, Nonna, " Massimo spoke with his eyes still closed so that he missed the glare that Nonna sent him. "But whoever she is, she's a good-looking woman. That red hair! I could really go for a woman with red hair."

"Too skinny," Nonna said.

✦ ✦ ✦

She had arrived three weeks ago, driving a battered green rental car, armed with a letter to Mayor Biasi. She'd been received graciously, with ill-concealed curiosity. There hadn't been a stranger in Malafortuna for nearly a hundred years and the news of her arrival was digested in every house along with their midday snack.

It *was* really out of the way. She'd gotten lost twice over steep mountain passes filled with stunted trees and unearthly beauty. And then, at the top of a hill, she pulled into a clearing. She could look down an entire mountainside and see the little farms and fences and a town below her. The road wound around and around, like the stripe on a candy cane. If she looked one way, she could see where she had just come from, and if she looked the other way, she could see where she would go. By the side of the clearing, she saw the worn sign that pointed the way down the mountain. She shifted into first gear and began the dizzying descent down.

The town itself was charming, with pink and yellow and white stuccoed houses, a little dilapidated to be sure, but decorated gaily with flowers spilling out of every corner and colorful laundry flapping from the windows. She drove into the square and managed to locate the Mayor's house. His wife, a cheerful round-faced woman who spoke English in a halting manner, exclaimed *"America!"* and told Julie all about the three cousins on her mother's side who had moved to America fifty years before. "We never hear from them," her bright face dimmed for a moment, "But one day, I know they gonna come back, no?" Julie nodded, happy to understand what the Mayor's wife had said to her. Maybe it wouldn't be so bad. Maybe everyone could speak a little English and the Italian that she'd spoken with her family since childhood would see her through. Lord knows, she'd been practicing every minute since she'd decided to make the trip to Malafortuna. So far, she'd understood everything everyone said, except for the one man at the restaurant in Salisi. Signora Biasi began chatting over her shoulder, as she brought Julie into the Mayor's study, and Julie felt as if she'd landed on another planet. What was the woman *saying?* It had to be the Malafortuna dialect. Nonetheless, the Mayor's wife was so happy and bouncy that she and Julie couldn't stop laughing over their attempts to converse with one another.

Mayor Biasi looked like a storybook caricature of an Italian administrator, with a great, bushy mustache, curling up to two ferocious points at either end. He sat, rubbing his hands together and eyeing her with admiration. Julie was relieved to find that she understood the Mayor's Italian and that he also spoke English rather well. "I can speak a little Italian, but not much," she confessed. "I've been using language tapes and trying to improve."

"You speak very well." He bowed his head toward her. "And what you don't know, ha, you will know in four days. Is no problem at all, lovely lady," his bright eyes gleamed. "Almost everyone, except maybe old ones who live here, speaks pretty good English. All the children, they learn in school." He patted her hand and raised his bushy eyebrows in sincere admiration of her long, beautiful American legs.

After hearing that she wanted to live here and learn how to cook, he left her with a cup of coffee and his wife, and went straight to Massimo. "Is it legal that she stay here?"

"Why not?" Massimo shrugged. "I don't think there's anything against it in the Regulation Manual, and anyway," his big shoulders hunched, "who cares? She could rent the second floor of Marina Corbone's house and give Marina a little company and income."

"As long as it's not against the law." The Mayor was glad that she would be staying; there were little enough good-looking women around. And he'd done his duty. If there were any problems from the authorities, he could now refer them to Massimo.

And so Julie settled in. At first, no one could believe that anyone like her could come halfway around the world to see the ways that people baked and cooked in Malafortuna. "Who could care how we cook?" asked Nonna Graziella. "We cook like we always cooked."

"That's why she's here," said Massimo who had already spent several hours with Julie and felt that he knew all about her. "She wants to go back to her family's roots."

Nonna Graziella snorted and sucked on the inside of her cheek. "Roots!" She said. "Roots! Huh! We go even deeper than that in Malafortuna. Here, we go right down to the bottom of the cesspool!"

✦ ✦ ✦

"My family thinks I've taken leave of my senses," Julie told Marina on the first afternoon, right after she'd seen the three tiny rooms at the top of the staircase that ran outside the house and agreed to rent them for what she thought was a minuscule amount of money. For an even smaller amount of money, Marina had offered to provide her with breakfast and supper every night. It was perfect, Julie thought, a new friend and a place to stay, all in one. After a few fumbles, which everyone found amusing, Julie found her

Italian was adequate for general conversation. Words she didn't know – well, she managed to sketch them out with her hands – and this seemed to endear her to the townfolk. They, in turn, fumbled with English, and then laughed at their own errors. They managed to understand her and she managed to understand them. It would all be fine.

"So here I was," Julie continued over cups of tea on Marina's scrubbed kitchen table, "in the biggest city in the world, clutching my diploma in my hand. There were eight job offers, each one better than the next, each one offering me obscene amounts of money to cook light fish lunches on decorated plates for their executives. But it wasn't what I wanted." She shook her head and Marina's head followed from side to side. "I was tired of the whole rat race." Marina's eyes widened a little at the new phrase. "I wanted to be somewhere quiet, where things were peaceful. Where there was no pretense, no trendy restaurants with people waving handfuls . . . handsful? . . . oh, well, you know what I mean, lots of money to get a good seat. Somewhere where nothing happened."

Marina digested all of this, delighted to welcome this attractive new person. She thought she understood. "You've certainly come to the right place," she said dryly, "Nothing whatsoever ever happens in Malafortuna."

"That's what my Grandpa said. He remembered *his* father saying that Malafortuna was the tail end of the universe. He said that if I wanted a dose of grit and reality, this would be a good testing ground."

"Well, I'm happy you're here," Marina's voice was warm. "I can use the rent money and it's wonderful to have someone new around here. Someone my own age to talk to." She sat back. "Now, tell me all about yourself."

"I'm twenty-six," Julie started. "Divorced." Marina made a face but didn't interrupt. "I grew up in a very happy family. My mother is Irish-Italian and my father is all Italian. I have one brother, Moe. His real name is Mauritzio and my real name is Giulietta, but everyone calls me Julie. The town I grew up in was near New York City, but still a nice small town. I went to college and then married a man named Stephen Stanton. He was the man of my dreams, I thought, but, after a little while, I realized that my dreams were all bad ones." Marina's face was sympathetic and Julie went on. "We divorced after two miserable years and then I decided to take up cooking so that I could keep busy and mend my broken heart." She laughed sheepishly and found that Marina was nodding in understanding.

"No babies?"

"No. And that was part of the problem. I was dying to have a baby. Then I found out that Stephen didn't want any children," Marina made a tutting sound and Julie found herself spilling almost everything, telling her things she never dared to say to anyone else. She couldn't seem to stop talking.

"I understand a little," Marina assured her when she finally wound down. "I, too, was married to a man who was bad. I still am, actually, divorce being nearly unobtainable here. He lives somewhere in Rome. Once in a while I hear about him, but I haven't laid eyes on his in, oh, let me see . . . over twelve years now. Tonio--Antonio--our son, doesn't remember him at all. He's never sent us any money, not even a letter to Tonio-- nothing!" She shrugged and watched Julie's expressive face nodding in comprehension. "You understand how it was. He was handsome and I loved him. I thought it was enough." Julie's face softened in sympathy. " My mother tried to warn me. My Nonna tried to warn me. My brother tried to make me change my mind. But I was stubborn. I only wanted Paolo." She made a face and Julie laid her hand over Marina's small brown one.

"And so we got married. My dowry bought this house," she gestured in the air. "In two days, I realized what a fool I had been, but what could I do? This is Italy and this is Malafortuna. I had to live with my mistake. Fortunately, right after Tonio was born, Paolo left us for a gayer life," Marina's face smiled as Julie snorted. "But I had Tonio. He's my whole life, my sunshine, although the boy is turning into a rascal," she shook her head, rue battling with the pride in her voice. "He'll be here soon and you will meet him. He's almost fourteen and needs a man's hand to guide him. He's at that age where he's bored at school and he's beginning to make a little trouble, nothing serious, but he needs a firmer hand than mine."

"You've not met anyone else, then?"

"Who could I meet here? Everyone with a brain leaves Malafortuna the day that they can. There are no eligible single men here . . . well, there are a few. Massimo, our village policeman is single," she started to laugh infectiously and Julie chuckled with her. "Anyone who takes on Massimo takes on his mother and his grandmother too! And the rest? No, there's no one here for me." She stood up and began to clear the cups from the table. "You wanted the ends of the earth, Julie. You've certainly found them here."

✦ ✦ ✦

Julie folded her clothes and put them away. The little apartment was sparsely furnished, but there wasn't much that she really needed. She was unpacked and done in a few moments. Other than clothing, she hadn't brought too much with her. The sun shone through the open windows and the little terrace at the top of the steps was filled with terra cotta pots of flowers and herbs. "I love it," she said out loud. She washed off the dust of travel in the antiquated tin bathtub, put on a clean pink shirt, a blue denim wrap-around skirt, and slid her feet into leather sandals. She propped up the old gilt-edged mirror she had found lying on a dresser and brushed her coppery hair until it stood out like a bell around her head. She heard a gong ring downstairs and she trotted down, hungry as a wolf, to enjoy her first taste of Malafortuna cuisine.

She knocked lightly on Marina's back door and walked in. The round table now boasted a bright tablecloth, and pottery dishes were set for three. She sniffed in rapture. "It smells wonderful! What can I do to help?"

Marina turned from the stove. "Nothing tonight. Tonight, you are our new guest. After tonight, you are still our guest, but not so new and you can help out a little." Marina was tiny and curvy with glossy black hair wrapped around her head in a coronet. Her eyes were dark and shiny and her pretty face was wreathed in a smile. "You want to learn to cook, we'll let you!" She stirred a handful of salt into the pot of boiling water and peered into the oven. "Tonio! Supper's ready!" The steam from the pot made a few wisps of her hair fall down around her face and Julie thought she was one of the prettiest women she'd ever seen.

Tonio was tall and gangly, with his mother's raven hair cut in a ragged fashion. His eyes were dark, lavishly lashed, and he was at that stage of adolescence where nothing grew quite at the same time. He all but gawped at her and Julie grinned. It was obvious that when his parts came together, he was going to be a heartbreaker. "Hi, Tonio. I'm Julie." She gave him a little wave.

"No! No!" Marina protested. "You are Mrs. Stanton. Our guest." Tonio's handsome young face took on a mulish look that Julie remembered from her own childhood.

Julie took his hand in hers. "I'll be your guest, but I want to be Julie to both of you. Please."

Tonio's face blushed rosy, but he managed to gather his manners about him. He bowed over her hand, "Plizzed to meet you, Julie." His English was a little awkward, but, Julie acknowledged, so was her Italian. He smiled at her with dazzling white teeth. Marina hugged him fondly and he shrugged her off, clearly embarrassed at her show of affection in front of a stranger. And a pretty woman stranger at that. A mother should not do that to a boy . . . almost a man.

"Sit down. Sit down." Marina caught Julie's eye. Julie slid into the chair that she'd used in the afternoon and Tonio threw himself down into another. "Julie is from America and she'll be staying with us, upstairs, for a few months." Tonio nodded, picking up a piece of bread from the basket on that table and stuffing it into his mouth. Marina cleared her throat and made a motion with her head. "Perhaps you'll serve our guest first, Tonio."

Mortified as only a teen-aged boy could be, he put the bread back on his plate and passed the basket to Julie. She took a piece and began to talk, trying to ease the tension. "This bread is fantastic. Look at the texture! The crust! Did you make this, Marina?"

Marina shook her head and the tiny earrings in her ears danced. "No. Bread is something the baker makes best. The ovens they have . . . We really can't do it at home. Tonio goes every morning before school down to Sopa's Bakery and brings me what I need for the day and enough for his *panini* . . . sandwiches, you say in English, for his lunch at school." She ladled soup into their bowls. "Julie is here to learn to cook our way," she said to Tonio. He looked incredulous. "It's true," she said to him, laughing. "Imagine that! All the way from America to see what we do here! So, I will explain about everything we eat." He nodded doubtfully and picked up his spoon. Warily, he watched until Julie picked her spoon up. Marina looked pleased.

Julie sipped at the soup. It was a golden broth, with tiny pieces of meat floating in it. "Gorgeous!" She breathed and then tipped her head to one side. "Chicken broth?"

"Veal and chicken. Left overs. The meat is veal." Tonio scraped the bottom of his bowl and cautiously took another piece of bread, his liquid eyes watching to see that Marina approved.

Dinner was a roll of pounded chicken breast, wrapped around thin slices of cheese and ham, served on a bed of *orzo*. "We call this '*uccellini*' - little birds," Marina explained as they ate. "In really olden days, instead of chicken, we'd use a tiny bird, a thrush, but no one now, except the old men who live out on the farms, can get enough birds any more." She laughed, "I said nothing changes in Malafortuna, but I suppose some things change, even here."

"Not much, though," said Tonio, looking glum.

Julie was starving and the food was delicious. The flavors were sharp and simple, each ingredient complimenting the others. She smacked her lips in delight and then told them stories about some of the things that were being served in the United States and being passed off as Italian cooking.

Marina was stupefied. "*Pineapple* ravioli! No. Surely you are joking? No?"

"I don't think I'd like that," Tonio said, giving Julie a lopsided grin. "But, everything else in America, I would like. The trains, the fast automobiles, the airplanes -- everything!" He pushed his plate away and sat back. Marina began to clear the table and Julie got up to help.

"Not tonight, Julie. Tomorrow night, perhaps. But tonight, please, no." Julie sat down as Marina whipped the dishes off the table and stacked them by the big old-fashioned sink. She brought a platter of peaches to the table. Julie picked up a peach and smelled it. It was at its peak of ripeness, nearly bursting in her hand. Its perfume was enticing, actually making her mouth water.

Tonio watched her enjoyment and at a sharp look from his mother, jumped up to get fruit plates and fruit knives. Julie picked up a knife. "You guys are much more civilized than us when it comes to fruit. We just bite out a chunk." She held the knife awkwardly, cut off a piece and tried to eat it neatly. The juice spurted and ran down her chin. She laughed and mopped herself off. "I'm such a sloppy person!" Tonio's mouth was open and he looked at her with adoration. Marina smiled to herself and brought the coffee to the table.

"The peaches come from Zio Nunzio's farm, down the road. He breeds goats too, and he swears that the goat manure makes the peaches extra sweet." Tonio choked in embarrassment to hear his mother talk about goat manure. He had to be thumped on the back, which made him even more embarrassed.

Julie laughed out loud, trying to make him comfortable. She could feel his adolescent admiration and sensed it would be best to treat him like a younger brother. "My uncles and my father worship their manure too. It must be in the blood." She watched him deftly skin his peach, then cut it into small pieces. "I'll have to watch to see how you cut your fruit. I want to learn everything." Tonio dropped four cubes of sugar into his coffee cup. Marina did the same. Julie watched them. "Everyone does things differently," she mused. "Not better, not worse, just different. For instance, I drink my coffee with cream, but no sugar." Marina jumped up, horrified that she hadn't put out any cream and Tonio and Julie wagged their eyebrows together over her distress. "Thanks, Marina. I guess that's the way I do it." She sipped at her coffee. "Maybe one day I'll try it your way. That's why I'm here." She saluted them with her cup and took another whole peach from the plate. This time, she bit right into it's pink and gold flesh, rolling her eyes in ecstasy as the juice spurted all over her chin.

✦ ✦ ✦

A typical breakfast in Malafortuna, Julie learned the next morning, was a bowl of coffee, half filled with milk, almost the way she'd drunk it the night before. Tonio had already been to the bakery and there were several crisp hot rolls at the table, as well as toasted stale bread from the night before. Julie ate all of the fresh rolls, unable to stop herself, while Marina and Tonio preferred the toasted bread, spread with jam and dipped into their coffee bowls. Marina was astounded to hear about bacon and eggs and waffles and pancakes. "How could anyone eat so much so early in the morning?" she wondered.

Tonio waved and went off the school. Julie ate the last roll while Marina told her about her own family and some of the people who lived in the valley.

"My name before I was married was Alessi, and there have been Alessis here in Malafortuna since the time when the valley was settled hundreds and hundreds of years ago. My father is dead, but my mother, Sofia, lives in the yellow stone house, three doors away from the church. Her mother, my Nonna Caterina, lives there with her. My father was the town barber, and his father was the town barber and so forth back into history. My brother, Alessandro, however, no longer lives here, so the job of barber went to someone else." She laughed, "God forbid that anyone might have suggested to Alessandro that he be the town barber!"

"What's wrong with being a barber?" asked Julie. "The men in my family have been garbage collectors since they came to America and no one is ashamed of it." She thought briefly back to her last dinner date in New York. She'd be sure to tell Marina about it one of these days and maybe they could laugh together over the story.

"Nothing. There's nothing wrong with being a barber, only you'd have to know my brother to appreciate how far he's distanced himself from anything in Malafortuna, much less a barber chair!" She saw Julie's face and continued. "Alessandro was always a little bit different from the other boys here. He was the smartest and most ambitious boy in town. He won a big scholarship, worked hard, and went to the University of Bologna, graduated with the highest honors, and then started his own company." Her round face took on an odd expression, a mixture or pride and exasperation. "Alessi Limited is now a huge corporation. They supply Ferrari . . . you know the Ferrari car, no?" Julie nodded. "Well, Alessi supplies them with their precision engines. Alessandro is the head of the company and a very important man. The dynasty of Alessi barbers came to a halt when Alessandro was born."

"Your mother must be very proud of him," Julie offered.

"Yes." She drew the word out slowly, as if she wasn't quite sure. "But he doesn't come now to see her much. I think he feels Malafortuna is, how shall I say this? A little backwards for a man such as himself."

"Is he nice?"

"Oh, he's wonderful. So intelligent. So well-dressed. So wealthy. And so many people work for him." She beamed with pride and Julie thought that brother Alessandro sounded like a real asshole.

"Tell me some more about Massimo Nulla." She didn't want to hear any more about the enviable Alessandro Alessi. He sounded too much like someone she'd really dislike, and she loved Marina already and wouldn't want to hurt her feelings.

"Massimo." Marina poured herself a little more coffee and then added hot milk. "Let's see. There are two Nulla brothers. There are a couple of other Nulla cousins, but most of them went to live in America. They live somewhere near Chicago, I think. Anyway, the ones here are the ones you need to know about. Massimo is the older and Renzo is a year or two younger. Renzo grew up with Alessandro, and the two of them were inseparable until Alessandro went away to school. Renzo is married to a nice local girl, Carmella, and they are settled here. He's a musician and has a band that plays on the last Friday of every month in the village square. Everyone in the village goes to listen and dance. It's the highlight of the town's social life, which can give you another idea of how dull things are here," she laughed and continued. "But Massimo never married. He's very handsome." Marina's face grew a little pink, "and he's lots of fun. He always has two or three girls who are hopeful, but he's a *mammoni*.

"A what?"

Marina's dark eyes were impish. "A man who lives with his mother. Who will *always* live with his mother. Why? Because no one could be as good to Massimo as she is. He has such a good situation there. *La mamma* cooks for him. Cleans up after him. Catches his shirt before it hits the floor and washes it, dries it and folds it away for him. She makes sure his bed is soft and that there is always good food and cold wine for him to drink." She giggled at Julie's open mouth. "But no! Not like that! He's a normal man." Again, Marina's cheeks grew hot and pink. "More than a normal man. He adores women, so watch out, Julie. He's very sexy, magnetic, and all the women are dying to become his wife. Only they never will. Why? Because he has his mother. *And* his grandmother, Nonna Graziella. They wait on him hand and foot. Why would he ever want to leave?"

"Doesn't he want a wife? A family?"

Marina shrugged and Julie glimpsed something down in the depths of her dark eyes. "I guess not. As I said, he has nearly any woman he bats his gorgeous eyelashes at. Ha! His mother introduces him to every woman in the area. She probably urges him to sleep with some of them." Marina looked at the tablecloth and drew a circle around and around with the tip of her spoon. "But Massimo always comes home to Mamma after everything is over. No woman - no one - could take care of him like she does."

"Amazing!" Julie shook her head. "Such a waste of a good-looking man!" She tried out the new word, "*Mammoni,*" and rolled the word around in her mouth, savoring it. "And who else lives here?" She couldn't wait to hear more.

"Teodora Sopa, the bakerwoman. I guess I should tell you about her and Zara Pomafilla."

"Tell me." She put her elbows on the table and leaned forward.

"Teodora grew up around the corner from our house. She was always shy. Stayed by herself a lot and always had to work at her mother's bakery. When she reached sixteen, she went away." Marina shook her head. "That's not so unusual. Nearly everyone goes as soon as they can. Well, anyway, Teodora left, and then, three years later she came back and took over the bakery when her mother died. She brought back her little daughter, Chiara, who is about Tonio's ago now. No one knows if she was ever married or not. She doesn't discuss that part of her life with anyone, and once or twice, if some of the real gossips have tried to find out, she freezes them completely."

"Not so unusual in America," Julie said, I have lots of friends who have children and no fathers or husbands."

"Here too, it's not such an unusual thing. We pretend it's unusual, but then, in Italy we pretend a lot of things." Marina continued drawing her imaginary circle on the tablecloth. "But Teodora's story has a little more than just that," Marina went on. "When they came back, Teodora also had a friend with her, another woman named Zara. Zara works at the bakery and lives with them. Again, no one is invited to ask, but the entire village thinks that they are lovers, Zara and Teodora."

"Oh," Julie said.

"Just so you know," Marina made a gesture with her chin.

"Thank you. Otherwise I might say something stupid, although I have several friends who are gay. Men and women both. Again, it's not so unusual in America."

"Maybe in America, but here, well . . . there is always talk. The people here are nice people, for the most part, but there are some who will always look sideways at them. Me? I like them both. They run their business well, make good bread, take good care of Chiara . . . the rest, well, who cares?" She shrugged her shoulders emphatically. "I think I can tell you this in confidence and you won't breathe a word," Julie leaned even further over the table, eager. "I think Tonio likes Chiara, you know, like a girlfriend." Julie bit at her bottom lip and a big grin split her face. "He always finds excuses to run to the bakery, but he'd hate it if I said anything. He's so touchy nowadays. This is such a difficult age for him . . . and for me."

"Being a teenager is hard anywhere. Some of my cousins and their kids-- I wonder how they make it through these years!"

"Tonio is a good boy," Marina's sweet face was earnest. "But without a father, it is very hard. He knows everyone in Malafortuna knows that his father deserted me." She made a face, "I wish Alessandro would take more of an interest in him, but they don't seem to have anything in common," her voice was wistful and Julie wanted to smack Alessandro on the side of his apparently swelled head.

"Who lives in the big house next to City Hall?"

"Otto Zampone, currently the richest and stingiest man in Malafortuna. He came from nothing, his father was the village bum when he died and his poor mother died from shame a few weeks later. Otto worked for his Uncle Gaetano at Gaetano's farm over on the hill. They deserved each other." Marina's face was scornful. "Two miserable men, living in squalor and hoarding every *lire*. They hated everyone in the village and no one wanted anything to do with either of them. When the old man died, Otto became his heir. He sold all of the hillside farm and land to some weasel of an attorney in Torriano and I understand that they are advertising in the English papers to sell the properties. "Tuscan Villas" they call them to the fools who live in London. Malafortuna is nowhere near Tuscany, I don't understand why they call them Tuscan at all!"

Julie laughed out loud. "What *is* it about the word "Tuscan" that makes people believe anything?"

Marina's shoulders and eyebrows rose. "Who knows? Tuscany is more than three hours away from here!" Julie shook her head. "Ah, people are gullible. Especially the rich. No one has bought anything yet, and everyone is waiting to see what will happen there." She dusted off her hands and stood up. "So, now you know a little about your neighbors, good and bad. Tomorrow we can gossip some more. This has been such fun for me, Julie. I rarely get to talk with someone my own age. Ah, well, I have to get to work." Marina worked as a receptionist in Dottore DiZito's offices. "I'll walk with you and you can spend the day with my mother and Nonna Caterina. They're dying to meet you and make lunch for you. When you're through, they'll bring you to the office. Mamma always has a question or two about her feet for Dr. DiZito, and she'll love the excuse to pop in."

Julie ran upstairs to get her notebook. She gave her hair a quick brush, washed her hands and made sure she looked neat and clean in the mirror. She ran back down the stairs feeling as excited as a kid going to a carnival. Who could have imagined that she'd feel so happy here?

CHAPTER FOUR

After two weeks, Julie felt completely at home in Malafortuna. She had spent several mornings with Sofia and Nonna Caterina learning how to cook their special dishes. She knew a lot more about Marina's brother, or, as she privately called him, "Saint Alessandro", and how he was too busy and too important to come visit his mother, his grandmother, or to pay any kind of attention to his sister and her as-good-as fatherless son.

She'd spent delightful hours at the bakery and found Teodora and Zara astonishing in their abilities to turn out remarkable breadstuffs, day in and day out, with only their old stone ovens and no commercial equipment to make their work easier. "If we had all that newfangled stuff, Julie, the bread wouldn't taste as good," Teodora explained to her. She'd met Chiara on her second day there and caught Tonio poking his head into the bakery a few times, blushing every time he saw her. Chiara was a darling girl, and obviously as adoring of Tonio as he was of her.

She'd met Zio Nunzio and his wife, Zia Nina, and been personally introduced to their entire herd of pedigreed goats, one by one. Zio Nunzio asked her if she knew his nephew Orazio who lived in Cincinnati. "I 'tink he's a shoemaker. Do you know him?" Sorrowfully, Julie shook her head. She didn't know too many shoemakers in Cincinnati, unfortunately.

She'd spent an afternoon with Massimo's mother and Nonna Graziella. The two ladies thawed enough in their estimation of her to have invited her back next week to watch them make *Rosolio*, the fiery, ruby red liquor which was their specialty, and which they'd never let anyone else watch them making. Massimo agreed that she had made a hit with them and warned her that his mother was making noises that she wanted Julie as a daughter-in-law.

"I don't think so, Massimo," she told him as she walked away, "I don't share my men."

"Promise me at least two dances!" he yelled after her and she waved her hands in the air to show that she had heard him. Such an enigma, Massimo was, she thought. In America, he'd be derided as a Mamma's boy, but here, it was almost a badge of blazing manhood that he kept such a harem and yet lived at home. Handsome, virile, and seemingly as lazy as a hounddog, Massimo could probably have any girl in the valley, she mused, and in reality, most had succumbed to his advances. He had a prized Italian Government job, and being a policeman in the backwater of Malafortuna didn't appear to put any strain whatsoever on his indolent, aimless days. His startling blue eyes, surrounded by lavish, spiky lashes, contrasted with his smooth, olive skin and he skillfully flirted with Julie just a little. Enough to make her know that he would flirt with her a lot more if she gave him any encouragement. She liked him enormously. He made her laugh, but there was no spark between them. She'd give her right elbow, however, to bring him to New York and introduce him to Mariah.

Almost everyone had been so nice to her; everyone except Otto Zampone, who spit on the ground when she was introduced to him, muttering something about foreigners. "He's nasty to everyone," Marina stuck her tongue out at Otto's retreating back. "He's always been a horrid man. Don't let him spoil Malafortuna for you."

"I wonder why he hates Americans?"

"He hates everybody. He's stingy and mean and glares at everyone. I used to be terrified of him and his uncle when I was a child. The old miser! They say he has every coin he ever earned, plus every coin that Zio Gaetano ever earned. Nonna says he's cheated and lied and that Otto is so mean he'll try to take the coins with him when he dies."

"I'll just stay out of his way," Julie sighed. "And anyway, I don't think he could teach me anything about good cooking."

And already her first notebook bulged with recipes and ideas and she felt satisfied that coming to Malafortuna had been a great idea. The only disturbing incident occurred on Monday, when she came home to find her little terrace all but destroyed. Someone had overturned all her flowerpots, uprooted the *basilico* and *oregano* plants. Shards of broken pottery and dirt were all over the tiles of the floor.

Five minutes later, Marina dragged Tonio up the stairs by the nape of his neck. "Why did you *do* such a thing?" she cried, slapping at his shirt and cuffing him on his head.

Sullenly, not meeting their eyes, he told them that he'd had a terrible day in school. The *professore* screamed at him because he hadn't finished his homework. "Why?" the *professore* had asked in front of the whole class, "Perhaps because of the pretty American lady that now lived with your mother? Heh? Was he now too good to do his homework? And why wasn't he a better student like his Uncle Alessandro, heh?" Tonio sheepishly confessed that he didn't know what to say and the whole class had laughed at him.

He hung his head, unable to look at either of them. "I am so sorrow, Julie," he finally muttered in his halting English. "I don't know how it comes over me. I was so angry. I came home and before I knew what I was doing, I smashed everything up here."

Marina was furious with embarrassment. He'd shamed her in front of her guest. She boxed his ears again, standing nearly on tiptoe to reach him, slapping him until he cringed away with tears in his eyes. "You little animal!" she screamed. "You'll be punished for this! You'll clean everything up here and work for Julie every day after school for two weeks. No football! None of your rascal friends! No nothing! You march home from school and every day, you do just what Julie wants you to do, clean her floors, scrub her toilet, whatever!" She shook him, helpless in her anger and mortification and Julie was wise enough to say nothing until Marina burst into tears and stormed downstairs.

"Pliss, Julie, forgive me," Tonio was crying too, trying to snuffle back his tears. Julie gathered his skinny body into her arms somehow. She rocked him back and forth. Sniffling, bit by bit, he told her about his shame that his father deserted them. How he hated school and what a poor student he was. "They think my uncle was the Christ Child himself," he muttered rebelliously, and Julie had to muffle a chuckle. "It only makes me want to puke when they compare me with him." He drew himself up and tried to gather his dignity about him. "But is no excuse, Julie. I am shamed at what I did."

"I'm no saint, Anton," she told him, and he looked blankly at her. Anton? She shook her own head, perplexed. "I don't know why I keep calling you Anton in my mind. I know your real name is Antonio and everyone calls you 'Tonio'. I guess it's because we have a lot of Antons in my family and it's almost the same word." She kept talking, letting her words run on easily, giving him a chance to relax a little. "My father's name is Anton, and *his* mother's name was Antonina and *her* father's name was Anton and he was a Count a long time ago in Italy." He was listening closely and she deliberately kept her monologue flowing. "And don't feel bad that your father deserted you. One of the Antons in my background was born out of wedlock, and the other one, the Count, fathered my great-great grandmother, even though my great-great-great grandmother was married to someone else. And I made a big mess of my own marriage. Now!" The boy was trying hard to follow what she was saying. "Now, you know a little about my family's skeletons. Everyone has somebody in their background who made a little mischief, and everyone, including me, has made a lot of mistakes in life."

"Is true, Julie?"

"Is true, sweetheart. We have lots of mistake-makers in our family past and more often than not, they were named Anton."

He grinned just a little, feeling a bit better. "Anton. It's a good, strong name. I like it." He savored the sound of it. "Can you tell me some stories about these Antons? Anton is a man's name, not like Tonio, who always sounds like a little baby. And a Count, eh? Anton." And then he remembered again what he had done and turned pink with shame.

She couldn't stand to see him so upset. "Let's talk while we clean up this mess, Anton, my boy," she said briskly, trying to cheer him up. "You can be Anton the Count when you're up here, OK? I'll adopt you as kind of a cousin and you can be the one who can carry on the family heritage of making a little mischief. Mind you, Anton, the old Count, was a very learned man who always did the best for everyone under his patronage. And my father is a very respected man in Derryfield. *And,* Antonina, my auntie, was a famous opera star. You have a lot to live up to if you take the name.

"OK. I do anything. I weel work hard for you, Julie. I promise. I do it."

"It's correct to say *'I'll* do it'," she said, correcting his verb tense. "That's the proper way to say it in English, Anton." She snapped her fingers as a solution came to her. "I know. You can come up here after school and do your homework and do it right instead of cleaning. But you can only speak to me in English, proper English, and I'll correct everything you say wrong." He watched her narrowly. What was she up to? "And then, in return, you'll correct my Italian and make me learn to *parlare correttamente, no?"*

"Sure," he said, grinning broadly. She was someone who understood things. He would do anything for her now.

She shook her finger at him. "And you have to finish your homework every day and do it right. You're no dummy, Anton," the new name seemed right and natural. "I know you can do well in school. Otherwise, you'll be stuck here in Malafortuna milking goats for Zio Nunzio, and that would be damn shame."

"I could go nowhere anyhow," he told her, biting his lip. His dark eyes were sad. "My mother will need my money to keep herself. She has no one else, you know." His voice quivered.

"We'll figure something out, Anton," she told him sincerely. "You do your part. Buckle down and study. I'll do something, I don't know what just yet, but it will turn out fine. I promise you, sweetheart. I promise you."

✦ ✦ ✦

While the newly christened Anton swept up the debris, for the next half-hour, Julie soothed Marina. "He's just a kid, a fine boy. You should know some of the mischief my cousins, my brother and I were up to when we were that age." Marina shook her head, refusing to be comforted. She was ashamed and her eyes were full of tears. Julie hugged her and said assuringly, "We're going to help each other, me and your reformed son now named Anton."

"Who?"

"Anton. Your son with the newly turned leaf," and she explained it all to Marina.

"Perhaps it may be a good thing to come from this after all," Marina said slowly. "He needs some hope and some help, and you, a stranger, he might just accept it from. Anton . . . " she tried out the new name. Perhaps a new name will give him some new responsibility." She shrugged. "I will try anything to make a good man of him."

The next afternoon, Tonio appeared promptly at her door after school had ended. The terrace was clean, the plants repotted, and he'd scrubbed Julie's kitchen floor before she could even blink. She made them both cups of coffee and they sat at the little green metal table in her kitchen and talked.

"'I told everyone in school that they must call me Anton from now on."

"*Veramente?*" Julie entered into the spirit of her plan wholeheartedly. *And besides,* she told herself, *I need to work on my Italian.*

"True. I told them a small lie, though. I said that I had discovered that one of my ancestors was a Count in the old days. Everyone was very impressed. Was that OK to do?" His eyes begged her.

"Hmmmm? *Non e giusto, ma, in questo situation, forse e okeydokey.*" She mangled her Italian as badly as he mangled his English. "It's not really the best thing, but I guess it's OK in this kind of a situation."

"Situazione," corrected her new teacher and she meekly repeated the word correctly three times before he was satisfied with her pronunciation.

As he left to go downstairs, she asked him playfully, "Are you going to dance with me on Friday night?"

"Dance with you? His dark eyes showed her what promise they held for his future years. Something warm, maternal and dormant bumped against her heart. "Of course, Julie. I would be honored to dance with you. But I regret that I am not such a very good dancer."

"I can help you. You may not know this, but I'm considered the ultimate Arthuressa Murray around Connecticut."

"Who?" he asked, bewildered.

"Wait," she put up one finger and went to her suitcase to get out her tape player. "We're going to knock their eyes out next Friday night."

"Say it in Italian," chided the teacher.

She wore a pale blue linen dress with spaghetti straps and a whirly skirt. Marina had on a yellow flowered dress. Julie helped her do her hair in a new way. "We look great!" They walked together in the special glowing twilight that the village boasted. The square looked magical to her, changed into a fairyland filled with small tables and chairs, with a low bandstand erected on one side. There were twinkling lights twined in the trees and everyone was dressed in party clothes. Waiters from the La Famiglia Ristorante slid deftly between the tables, serving drinks and little pottery dishes of olives and cheese.

Marina greeted everyone gaily and guided Julie to a table where Renzo's wife, Carmella was sitting. Carmella was obviously in the late stages of what Marina said was her fifth pregnancy. She was a bouncy woman with frizzy bleached hair and a huge smile. "I'm so glad to meet you at last," she said eagerly to Julie. "I want to ask you for the names of some American film stars."

At Julie's puzzled look, Marina explained that all of Renzo and Carmella's children had American or English film star names. Marilyn, Rock, Tab and Shirley. "You have a child named 'Rock'?" Julie asked in an awed voice.

"*Certamente,*" Carmella's laugh bellowed halfway across the square. "What do you think of James Dean Nulla, if it's a boy or Cher Nulla, if it's a girl?"

Julie opened her mouth like a fish and gasped. In a tiny voice she said, "How about Leonardo or Madonna?" and Carmella's big eyes opened wide in pleased consideration.

Renzo and two of his band members stopped by the table and were introduced. He patted his wife's belly. "What do you think? We have already two of each kind. Boy or girl?"

"A girl," said Julie confidently after looking carefully at Carmella's bulge. "And don't laugh. I'm very good at this. Honest," she insisted when she saw their amused looks. "My great-great Grandma Mina was considered the finest *strega* in Connecticut. She could always tell and it's in my blood." she said proudly. "You wait and see. I really have the gift. I never miss!"

"I'd be a happy man if I had another little girl!" Renzo roared and Carmella beamed proudly. "It would be wonderful to have a house full of them, my little princesses." he winked at Julie, "And if you're right about it being a little *ragazza*, I'll make a special song for you." He waved good-bye and started to walk away, then turned back to the table, "Hey, Marina, I hear your brother will be here tonight."

"Ales*san*dro? Here?"

"Yeah. One of the boys saw him with his pretty red Ferrari at the rest stop on the *autostrada*. He said he was coming down 'cause it's your mother's name day today. OK! OK! " He waved at the stagehand who called to him. "I'm comin'. I'm comin'."

"Alessandro is coming here! I don't think Mamma knows. She'll be so happy that he remembered her name day." Marina looked to see if Sofia had arrived yet. "I don't see her, do you?" The band began to tune up and a raucous noise split the air as the amplifier misfired. The stagehand fiddled with some knobs and all of a sudden the air was filled with music. Bouncy, cheerful Italian music, and the crowd cheered and started to clap.

Renzo introduced his band and they swung into a version of "Volare". Zio Nunzio and the Mayor's wife began to dance. Julie was a little surprised at how well the two short, round people moved to the music. Mayor Biasi bowed to Zia Nina and they too went to the dance floor. Several other couples joined them and in a moment, Massimo was there, waving to his brother and bowing to Carmella to get up and dance. Bruno Bastingliata, the butcher, took Marina by the hand and Sammie Sanzarella, the seventy-five year old man who worked in the *farmacia* asked Julie to join him. The music played and darkness fell. Julie was having the time of her life. She danced with Massimo, who held her a little tighter than she was comfortable with, and then with Dottore DiZito and then with the Mayor. She was whirling around and almost missed seeing the group of three people who sat themselves at a table under one of the trees. Almost.

It was Sofia with Nonna Caterina, resplendent in a sparkly red dress, but . . . who? Who was *that*? Julie tried to turn the Mayor around a little bit so that she could see him better. *My word*! She whistled to herself, *it's got to be Alessandro The Great*. My Goodness Gracious! The man was gorgeous! He looked a little like Cary Grant, tall and darkly handsome, with a comma of unruly black hair that flopped over one eyebrow. His obviously expensive clothes fit his body beautifully. And those shoulders! He was stunning! Absolutely stunning. Naturally, Julie fastened her attention to the Mayor's flowery compliments and made sure that no one caught her looking at his table.

Alessandro Alessi courteously seated his mother and grandmother and then sat himself down, making sure that the creases in his Armani pants were straight. He glanced around, acknowledging the greetings of his former neighbors. He motioned one of the waiters to bring them drinks. "Me, I'll have a highball," said Nonna Graziella loudly. Alessandro winced. He knew Nonna did it on purpose.

He glanced casually at the dancers and then his head whipped back once again. Who in the hell was *that?* He turned his head carefully and watched her, dancing in fat Biasi's arms, her head thrown back, laughing at something the little squirt said to her. She was tall and slender, with a cascade of red hair that reflected the twinkly lights. He narrowed his eyes. She was smashing. Where in hell did she come from and what the hell was she doing in Malafortuna?

Nonna Graziella's eyes missed nothing. "She's from America."

"What? What are you saying?"

"The girl out there. She's an American." Nonna sat back with a smug look on her face. She paid no further attention to her grandson and interested herself in watching the dancers.

"What girl?" he asked with studied nonchalance.

Nonna made a funny sniffing sound with her nose and mouth and kept her back turned away from Alessandro. She loved him the best of all, but he was a royal pain in the ass sometimes. Sometimes, she wanted to slap him, the way he turned his back on his mother, his sister, and everyone. So he was smart. So he was handsome. It still didn't make up for treating all of them as if they lived in a pigsty. Let him stew for a while.

Renzo changed music, warbling a song about a man who loved pretty girls. The sweaty dancers stood on the edge of the dance floor clapping as he made up spontaneous rhymes using the names of the women in the village. He sang a verse about Carmella and everyone laughed when he made fun of her belly. He serenaded Zia Nina and made a joke about Zio Nunzio and the goats. He sang to his own mother--a stanza about his brother Massimo bringing home three brides at one time. The crowd loved it, and then Renzo stopped in front of Julie. He sank to his knees. The band stopped playing for an instant and then Renzo threw out his arms. His voice was a caressing whisper. He crooned that Julie came from the heavens of America and she was destined to cook *polenta* for some lucky man in Italy. Julie laughed out loud and Alessandro watched the lights as they made shadows on her white throat. Julie? Julie from America.

Sofia watched him from the corner of her eye. *Maybe . . .* she said to herself. *Maybe this one will make my beautiful son fall on his beautiful face and turn his calculator of a mind to mush. Maybe.* She prayed to her own personal saint. "Saint Sofia, make him fall in love and make a horse's ass out of himself. Please, dear Saint Sofia." A prayer to your saint on their name day was supposed to be very powerful. Sofia loved her successful son so much that it hurt. He was a wonderful son . . . well, he was wonderful in many ways. He just needed the right woman to soften him, make him think a little more like a human being and a little less like a business machine who made money. Maybe this Julie would be the one.

The music switched again to an Italian-American song, "The Darktown Strutters' Ball", and Alessandro groaned. The song represented everything he hated. Ginzos. Wops. Immigrants who spoka-da-Ennga-leesh. Oblivious to Alessandro's embarrassment over the song, and helped a bit by the three glasses of wine that she'd gulped, Julie stepped out onto the dance floor. Alessandro watched, his eyes narrowed. All by herself, the girl whirled out to the middle of the square and held out her hands to his nephew. Alessandro's handsome mouth dropped open, as thunderstruck as everyone else, as Tonio spun her around the dance floor. They jitterbugged. Pure American show-off swing dancing, flashy and intricate, their steps meshing and kicking. Tonio whirled her around and she ducked under his upflung leg. She waved her arms and her hips swung from side to side and her blue skirt twirled into the air, giving everyone a good glimpse of her long, shapely American legs. Tonio's face glowed with pride and you could tell that he knew everyone was watching them. The villagers stamped and yelled and there was naked envy in the eyes of every schoolboy watching Marina's son dance with the beautiful older American woman.

The song came to a crescendo and his nephew threw the girl up into the air, bounced her on his left hip and the swooped her up again and bounced her on his right hip. At the last chord, she was bent backwards, her coppery hair brushing the ground, and Tonio held her there while the whistles and clapping lasted for nearly two minutes. "Ju-Lee, Ju-Lee! An-Ton, An-Ton!" Alessandro had already figured out that her name was Julie, but who the hell was Anton?

Nonna Caterina cackled with glee. She whooped and got up to crush her great-grandson in a bear hug. Surprisingly, he hugged her back in front of the whole town and Marina almost wept at the unusual open show of affection. Alessandro kept his eyes on the girl as she laughingly brushed off two more invitations to dance and fell into a chair, her bosom heaving with exertion. She grabbed at a glass of wine and drank it down in one thirsty gulp.

"Enough of this, Ma," he was almost angry. "Who is she?" Sofia took pity on him, her great big successful son who had people bowing and scraping every minute of every day, and told him all about her. He tried to look around nonchalantly while his mother spoke, but his eyes devoured Julie. Nonna Caterina chuckled softly to herself.

He sat watching as the dancing intensified. He saw his nephew dancing with the little girl from the bakery and his mother's light steps as she waltzed with the Mayor. He waved to a few acquaintances and saw Nonna Caterina dance with Zio Nunzio. His sister danced twice with Massimo, making Nonna Graziella's eyes narrow. But mostly he watched the American girl. It was easy to watch her. She never sat back down again. She danced with Zio Nunzio, Massimo, and the Mayor one more time, and Alessandro noticed how deftly she pushed the Mayor's hand away when it slid down low across her hip. She danced with the butcher, with the man who sold milk and with Orazio Melillo, the elderly man with the cleft palate who tended Corsini's cows in the mountains. She'd only been there a few weeks and already, she fit into the life of Malafortuna better than he'd ever done.

He shrugged to himself; he'd never really wanted to fit into Malafortuna. Oh, certainly he'd been happy here when he was a boy, running wild with Renzo, terrorizing Corsini's cows, stealing peaches and teasing the girls. He and Renzo had been inseparable then, cutting their wrists one sunny afternoon and mingling their blood, swearing to be friends forever. Ah, those were childish days. Little boys grew up and he grew away from Renzo, the goats, his family and everything connected to Malafortuna.

He'd been brilliant, quickly outstripping the abilities of the teachers at the local school. The University stimulated his thirsty mind and the bright lights, well-cut suits and the luxuries of success seduced him until he grew ashamed of everything and everyone in his modest background. A pang of disquiet hit him as he watched his sister dancing serenely with Zio Nunzio. He loved Marina and wished she wasn't still tied to that *stronzo* she married. He'd tried to tell her, but . . . she'd been lofted with the promise of love and nothing he said had made any difference. He still ached for her problems when he bothered to think about her. Shit, he mused, he loved them all, but they just didn't fit into his way of life anymore. His conscious pricked at him. *Only because you made it a point to turn your back on them*, it said to him. All alone at the table, he shrugged. *I come here once in a while*, he defended himself. *I bring them presents and try to get them to come to the city with me. Spruce themselves up.* His conscious threw up its hands and turned away from him, disgusted, and he tried to argue with it one more time. *They* want *to stay here and wallow in the old ways*! He had tried to give Marina and his mother money, tried to make them move, but both of them, in their own ways, were as stubborn as the mules who pulled the ice wagons. They'd both told him "no thank you" and seemed content with their Malafortuna lives. He shrugged his well-clad shoulders one more time and watched her dancing.

Renzo strolled among the dancers, playing his mandolin, and picked his way to Alessandro's table. "*Ciao*, my old friend. We miss you around here, you big shot, you. How are you, buddy?"

"Fine, Renzo. Everything is fine." He ignored the comment about being missed around here. "I see you're going to chain yourself down a little bit more with another beautiful baby."

"Such chains, 'Sandro. Like molten gold," his broad face grinned and he played a little tune and then asked, "When are you going to ask her to dance?"

"Who?" Alessandro asked sharply.

Renzo just laughed and walked away saying, "Last dance coming up before we break!" And the swoony sounds of "Anim' e Core" rose into the night.

He found himself standing next to her and put his hand under her elbow a split second before Joey Sottosanti did. "I'm Alessandro, Marina's brother. May I have this dance?" She smiled at him and he was startled to see how tall she was, only an inch or two shorter than he was.

"*Piacere*," she said, and moved her body with his, "I'm Julie Stanton, your sister's tenant from America, but I suppose you already know about me." His eyes locked with hers. She smelled like a fresh baked cake, sweet and delicious, and her grey eyes were shadows, speckled with reflected light. She was tanned and there were freckles sprinkled across the bridge of her nose and along the tops of her cheekbones. She stunned him. He wanted to have her so much that it hurt.

The music swooped and they bent together with it, their steps meshing and their arms wound loosely around each other. Julie could feel the eyes of every person in the square watching them with avid curiosity. The lady from across the sea and the big shot who left the village behind him. Her hand was on the curve of his upper arm. His jacket was smooth and taut and her palm felt hot. His huge hand engulfed her right one and there was a tingle where they touched that ran down her arm and ended somewhere in her stomach. There was old wives' tale in her family about the hot, tingling touch that meant true love, but she pushed the thought out of her mind. She didn't want to think of anything but the sensation of being in his arms. Her cheek touched the side of his chin and she bent her head a little more, so that no one could see that she'd bitten her bottom lip. She warned herself to stop being such a fool, but nonetheless, a warm puddle started to grow inside her and her heart began to beat faster.

He spun her around expertly and pulled her slightly closer in the turn. Her legs brushed his and she felt the power in his thighs. His hand, on the small of her bare back, felt hot, like a burning brand, and she fantasized that in the morning she'd be able to see the imprint of his fingers there. Their faces were close, her eyes on a direct level with his mouth and she could smell his expensive aftershave. She was almost mindless, caught in the music and his arms and when the dance ended, she stood slightly dizzy, not quite realizing that they had stopped dancing.

"Can we sit and talk?" She nodded, too shaky to say anything. He led her to a table at the end of the square, under the branches of a tree where it was dark. She sat down and he tapped a passing waiter, asking for two glasses of wine. "*Vino locale, perfavore?*" And then to Julie, "Is that all right?" She nodded and smiled a bit, thankful that he hadn't ordered a Merlot Reserve.

They talked warily, asking questions, getting to know something about each other. Julie told him a little about herself, touching briefly on her divorce and saying only that she had chosen Malafortuna because it was the town from which her great-grandfather came. "Everyone said it never changed and that was precisely what I was looking for."

"And it will never change," Alessandro agreed. "You'll be bored with it in three weeks and then you'll be glad to get back to decent civilization and cultured people." She said nothing and he continued to talk. He told her about his own divorce. "It was a mistake on my part. She was the wrong person for me. It was best that we parted." There was a brief bleak expression on his face, and then it was gone. Bitterly he said, "It took me millions of *lire* to get a civil annulment, but it was well worth it. Marriage! Such a trap. Never again." He flicked a bit of lint off his jacket and she watched his fingers, strong and thick, with wiry black hairs on the back of his wrists.

Without thinking at all, she blurted, "Why don't you visit here more often? Your mother would enjoy seeing you and your nephew could use a little manly support."

He eyed her with a wary look, suddenly angry at her intrusion of his life. "What an eager busybody you are!" She blushed uncomfortably, aware that she had impulsively stepped across the line. "It's really none of your business," he muttered stiffly, shamed that she had hit such a vulnerable spot. Her head snapped back and she *was* somewhat ashamed of herself. It *had* been an impertinent question. Why the hell had she opened her big mouth like that?

He sighed, then, patiently, as if he were talking to an imbecile, he answered, "My dear Julie, I hate everything about this place. Look around you. What do you see? Lazy louts, content to live their lives drinking homemade wine under the grapevines and tending to their goats. No one has an original thought. No one cares what their clothes look like. Look at them! My mother's dress dates back twenty years and she doesn't care at all!" Julie made an odd face as he continued, "And don't think I care nothing for them. I've wanted my mother to come to Milano ever since I started the company. She and Nonna could live in splendor there, want for nothing. They would have a big apartment, right in the best part of the city. They could have maids and people to scrub the floors for them. Cooks! They could eat out at good restaurants every night, not worry about making pasta from scratch, and have their hair done every day. But no, no, Julie, they *want* to stay in this hole in the mountains. They refuse to leave this miserable place!" His voice was rising and he looked around uneasily in case someone might see him losing control.

No one was paying them any attention. In a whisper he continued, "And my stubborn sister and her sullen son, they could also come to Milano. I could easily set them up." His face was earnest and sincere. "I clawed my way up the ladder and I am now a rich man. I have enough money for everyone in my family to live a good life. To be envied by others, to be cocooned in luxury. To . . . to be admired by those who count. Marina could get herself a divorce. I could arrange it. She's still pretty, even if she's a little overweight." He was intent on what he was saying and missed Julie's eyes narrowing sharply. "A good diet doctor could slim her down and he could get her hair cut decently. She could catch a rich husband who could give her furs and jewels and cars and her hands wouldn't be red and sore with housework. Tonio could go to a private academy, meet boys of good families." He stopped for a moment and noticed that Julie's hand had crept up to her mouth and that her eyes were a darker shade of grey. He sat back and shook his head a little. "Oh, why do I go on like this, ranting and raving?" He shrugged his shoulders, making the silken fabric ripple. "They don't even know what they're missing."

"You're ashamed of them, aren't you?" Her voice was soft and he only noticed that the shadows of the leaves dappled her shoulders. He could see the soft roundness that disappeared below. He swallowed thickly. Now here was a woman that he could parade on his arm!

"Ashamed? No, Julie, not that." He liked the sound of her name on his lips. "But certainly, I wouldn't want my business associates to see the chickens running in and out of Mamma's yard. No, I wouldn't want the Chairman of Ferrari to see my Nonna bent over, with her skirts tucked up, picking *chicoria* on the side of the road! Who would? I . . . I love them. I just wish they'd be more," he shrugged, "up to date. Improve themselves a little. Live a little less like Ginzo's from the Third Century. Why can't they make something of themselves?"

It could have been, she thought sadly. There had definitely been a spark when they saw one another and certainly when they touched. He was so handsome, with his thick black hair falling over his golden forehead and his eyes black pools surrounded by incredible lashes. And there really had been, for a moment, something touchable between them. It could have been. But now, nothing would come of it. Never. Never would she waste her time on someone like him. He was the very thing, Italian style, that she had run so far to get away from. Who would think she had almost let herself fall in love with an Italian Yuppie, First Class. The Ultissimo Italian Yuppie. She could almost weep. In her heart, the little warm puddle froze and broke away, shattered into a million sharp pieces of disgust. She stood up suddenly and he was startled.

"You know, Alessandro, when I first heard about you, when I first heard the things that people said about you, I thought you sounded like a selfish jerk." Her voice was soft. It took a moment for him to realize what she was saying. His head snapped back at her words. What? What did she mean?

Her voice was even more honeyed. "The more people spoke about you, the worse you sounded."

"Now, wait a minute . . . !" He began to get angry, but she shushed him and continued.

"Please wait, Alessandro." She said his name like a caress. "Wait. Wait. I was wrong, Alessandro." Her voice stroked and he smiled complacently. Of course she was wrong, the silly little fool.

"I really didn't understand," she said, running her fingernail along the top of his arm and lightly touching the warm skin of his neck. She shuddered, appalled at her want, frightened at the way she desired him, despite everything.

He sucked in his breath at her touch. Such a woman! She'd be his tonight. He turned his dazzling smile toward her and began to rise from his chair. Where could he take her? Not to his mother's house and not to her place over his sister's listening ears. Everyone would gossip. He needed to find a place where they could be alone . . . Ah, he'd think of something.

She pushed him back down gently and the sweet smell of her made him desire her even more.

She was all shadows and honey. "You're not just a selfish jerk,

Alessandro," she whispered intimately. His head nodded in complete agreement. "No." Her coppery hair fanned out as she shook her head from side to side. He smiled confidently at her and her voice became even more warm and close. "No, you're not that. You're an idiotic, superficial asshole. You're not fit to wipe your sister or your mother's shoes or to clean your Nonna's dirty apron. No. There isn't a person in this lovely little place, except maybe Otto Zampone, who isn't worth twenty of you," Her voice rose, higher and higher. "You Yuppie creep, you!" And once again, in the space of a few months, she picked up her wineglass and dumped it over her escort's head.

CHAPTER FIVE

The bright sunlight streaming through the window woke him and he groaned with the pain of a monumental hangover. The room spun and he staggered to the water jug on the dresser and nearly gagged as he gulped the cool water. *Santa Maria!* He clawed through his suitcase, grabbing the *paracet* bottle. He shook four of the tablets into his nerveless hands and swallowed them. He stood as still as he could while the room moved around him, tipping him into nausea. Retching, he fell back into bed. He closed his eyes, unable to stand the light and lay still until the medicine made it possible for him to open them again.

His suit and shirt were on the floor, stinking of wine and sweat and he tried to remember how he got back to Mamma's house. Renzo. Renzo had helped him stagger back after they both had gotten pig drunk when the dance was over. Renzo. God bless you, my blood brother and loyal good friend.

A cold bath, a shaky shave and three more tablets. He kicked his filthy clothes into a corner of the room, dressed himself in a clean shirt, dark blue slacks, and a fairly new off-white Armani slubbed silk jacket. He peered at his reflection in the mirror, shrugged and then winced as the top of his head felt the pain of his quick movement. He reluctantly went downstairs to face his mother's scorn and amusement.

Wordlessly, she put a cup of scalding black coffee on the table and he drank it, shuddering and trying to appear as normal as possible. Mamma plunked the bright blue *Brioschi* bottle down and spooned the yellow crystals into a glass of water. "Here," she said and held the foaming glass out to him. Keeping his eyes downcast, he took it and drank it down.

Nonna came into the kitchen, slamming the screen door and his brain split into a thousand pieces of pain. "Have a good time last night?" she asked brightly. He shrugged carefully, hoping that his head wouldn't fall off. Damned if he would tell either of them how horrible he felt.

He flipped out his portable telephone and dialed Signora LaMonica at the office. "I'll be in later today . . . yes, yes, I know. Tell her that I'll see her later tonight . . . Certainly . . . Goodbye." He turned back to the table and two pairs of eyes watched his every move. He clutched his tattered dignity about him. "Mamma, my clothes are upstairs on the floor. They're ruined." Nonna's eyes gleamed, but she had the sense to keep quiet. "Give the clothes to the poor." He stood up, suppressing a groan with difficulty. "I'll call you later during the week, Mamma. Goodbye." He bent and kissed her cheek. "Goodbye, Nonna Caterina," his eyes slid over her speculative ones and he kissed her too. Over the roar of the Ferrari's engine, the two women looked at one another and shook their heads.

He drove out of the square, racing the engine and just barely missing one of Signora Balducci's hens. The *Brioschi*, the little white pills and the coffee were all doing their job and he took a deep breath of late morning air. Perhaps his head wouldn't fall off after all.

He drove out of town, his hands careless on the wheel, then turned toward the road to Torriano where he'd hook up with the *Autostrada* to Milano. The gleaming red car roared past Zio Nunzio's farm and then, out of the corner of his eye, he saw her. He stomped on the brake and the powerful car slewed sideways, stopping inches away from Zio's fenced in pasture. She was in the field, walking toward the water trough carrying a baby goat in her arms. She stopped to watch as he got out of the car. She was wearing some kind of blue shorts low on her hips and a blue and white striped shirt was tied in a knot around her ribcage. His breath caught in his throat at the sight of her. He opened the gate and walked towards her and she stood still, staring at him.

The grass in the pasture was still damp with dew and he noted with a tiny corner of his brain that his shoes were going to be ruined. It was hot and he took off his jacket and slung it over his shoulder.

The goat bleated and she shifted her weight. Until the day he died he'd never forget how she looked. The sun was on her hair and it gleamed like a helmet. Her arms and legs were tanned and bare and he could see the flat planes of her stomach and the shadow of her bellybutton. For the first time in his life, he was speechless and he came up to her feeling like a twelve-year-old boy.

"What do you want?" Her grey eyes narrowed and she backed away slightly.

"I . . . I . . . ." He couldn't seem to string a sentence together. He just stood there with his mouth open like a codfish, he, who was the president of a huge corporation. She began to giggle at his mouth flapping uselessly and the baby goat bleated for its mother.

"Can't you talk today, Mister Bigshot? Got a little headache?" she taunted.

Damn this town, he swore to himself. Everyone knows everything! A man can't even have a little wine without the whole place gossiping! He tried to compose himself and put his foot up on the rim of the trough, striking what he thought could pass as an insouciant pose. "Um, I, um, wanted to talk to you," he managed to say. His poise was returning and he began to be angry with her. Who the hell was she to cause him to stammer like a bashful child? "Um, we, um . . . We seemed to, um, get off on the wrong foot last night," he began in his most seductive voice. "I'm sorry if you left with such a bad impression of me." He smiled the smile he used when he wanted to charm a difficult client. "I'm not such a bad guy when you get to know me." He tried his most melting smile. The one that never failed him with women. She tipped her head quizzically, listening to him blather on, and the little goat snuffled and nuzzled into her neck. He felt the power coming back to him, felt he was back on track now. He plowed on, "I, uh, wanted to know if you might have dinner with me some night this week." Her eyes slid across his face and she made a funny sound in her throat. She bit her lip and almost started to giggle. His black eyes narrowed and he stiffened. What was happening here? She made a whooping sound and her eyes danced. She couldn't stop it--a bubble of laughter popped out of her mouth.

"What?" he asked, a dangerous look coming into his eyes. She tried unsuccessfully to compose herself and he got madder and madder. What the hell was the matter with her? She sputtered, bending over with mirth and then began to laugh out loud. "What?" he roared furiously. "What's so damned funny?"

She dropped the little goat onto the grass and pointed. Then she bent over double, howling with laughter, curling her bare arms around her midriff, shrieking with glee. He whirled around and saw the mamma goat standing at his side, chewing contentedly on what was left of the sleeve of his expensive jacket.

"*Managia!*" He pulled hard at the jacket and the entire sleeve ripped, dangling out of the goat's mouth. "Baaaa!" cried the little goat and trotted over to its mother. The mamma goat swallowed convulsively and the rest of the sleeve of his jacket disappeared down her throat. She shook herself, completely unaware of his outrage, turned, calling to her little one. The two goats trotted off down the pasture, wig-wagging their stumpy tails.

"Ohhhhhh!" Julie cried, nearly hysterical with glee. He glared at her.

"My new jacket! My brand new jacket!" His fury made his eyes pop. "You think that's *funny!*" He stepped closer to her holding up the rest of the jacket. Helplessly, with tears streaming down her face, she nodded.

He was seized with a red-hot anger and he grabbed her and picked her up in the air as if she weighed no more than a feather. "Funny! You dare to laugh at me!" He whirled her around and then, goaded beyond thought, dropped her with a huge splash into the water trough. "Aha! Let's see how funny you think that is! How are you laughing now?" he roared.

She was a sorry sight, rump down in the water and her two bare legs with white sneakers on her feet sticking up in the air. She was completely drenched and pieces of grass and mud were plastered all over her face and hair. Her eyes blinked and she shook water and filth out of her hair. Her mouth was opened in a round "O" and he couldn't believe what he had done.

"Oh my God, Julie!" He was aghast. How could he have done something like this? With mortification, he stuck out his hand to help her up. "I didn't mean . . . I . . . I'm so sorry . . . ."

She grabbed onto his hand. He bent to pull her out. With a hard pull, she grabbed his hand, overbalancing him. With great glee, she pulled him, headfirst, into the trough with her.

He came up fast, like a man possessed, his dark hair plastered to his head, his face filthy and his shirt soaked. "You little devil, you!" he yelled, furious. And then he started to laugh too. Huge, bellowing yelps of laughter. He laughed so hard that he keeled over on the side of the trough, rolling back and forth in the mud, laughing and laughing and then he picked her up out of the water and plopped her into the mud next to him. "So! How do you like it now?" He giggled like a schoolboy and then he pushed her into one of the large mudpuddles. She floundered and squished. Laughing madly herself, she shoved at him and he slid further into the mess. The two of them, covered with mud and goat shit, collapsed hysterically in one another's arms, like two naughty children.

"Maybe there's something worth saving in you after all," Julie told him as he finally helped her stand up.

Zio Nunzio and Zia Nina watched them with astonished wide eyes, their mouths open and gaping. Within ten minutes, everyone in Malafortuna knew that there was a romance blooming.

CHAPTER SIX

"I still can't believe that you're going out to dinner with Alessandro." Marina sat on the edge of her bed, watching as Julie dressed to go out. "I just can't get over him taking anyone as nice as you out. Not that he ever talks much about his love life, but I get the impression that he only dates bimbos." She rolled her dark eyes.

"I hope I'm doing the right thing," Julie bent to see her reflection as she stuck the silver post of an earring into her lobe. "Now, how do I look?" She turned around slowly to give Marina a good look at her lightweight black suit. The skirt was long and straight and the top was scoop-necked and sleeveless. She wore a long silver chain around her neck and the earrings were simple circles of hammered silver that reflected bronze highlights from her hair. She looked cool and sexy, Marina decided, "Just right. And if you put on some shoes, you'll be perfect."

Alessandro changed clothes at his mother's house. He came downstairs; smelling of after-shave and both Sofia and Nonna Caterina nodded their approval. "You take good care of that girl!" Nonna cautioned him loudly as he left the house.

"I can't believe she didn't add to have you home by midnight," Alessandro groused as the powerful car cut through the night.

"She's concerned about my girlish reputation," Julie told him. "She knows I'm a simple village girl and you're a city slicker."

"What's that mean?"

"It's just an expression. It means that you're sophisticated and know the ways of the world and that I could be easily manipulated by your evil ways." He made a wolfish face and they both laughed. She turned her back against the car door and looked at his profile. He drove easily, manipulating the car around the hairpin twists and turns with careless grace. He smelled good, some citrus blend and she pushed the little frisson of eagerness back down. *Don't get over-excited*, she told herself. *He is a city slicker and he knows what he's doing - every little step of the way. Don't think too much about this date--he's only taking you out to dinner.* "Where are we going?"

"Luisa's Ristorante. It's in Torriano, the next village over the mountains, about 40 kilometers away. When you said you wanted authentic cooking, I immediately thought of Luisa. She's been standing behind that big black stove for years. I won't tell you any more except I know you'll enjoy yourself." He negotiated a difficult turn. "Afterwards, if you want, we can go dancing." She whipped a quick glance at his face, but all she could see was the dark shape of his head in the greenish lights of the dashboard. "Renzo and the band are playing in the Torriano square. They have these standing dates to play -- Torriano on the first Saturday night of every month and Malafortuna on the last Friday night. Big time entertainment here in the country."

"Good. I like Renzo and his band." Julie turned slightly and looked out of the window. It was pitch dark and she could barely see anything except her own reflection in the dark glass. Her copper hair looked like the night clouds and she couldn't see the expression in her own eyes. *Maybe just as well*, she thought. *That means he can't see what I'm thinking either*. She tried to keep the chatter on a light note. "Does Renzo work anywhere else? I mean, two nights' playing each month . . . It can't feed all those movie-star children."

Alessandro's laugh was warm and she felt as if the laugh wrapped itself around her shoulders. This was a dangerous person she was sitting with. "He works for a music publishing company. He does the musical accompaniment for singers to keep the brood fed."

"They seem like a happy family." She peered out of the window, fascinated by the brief glimpses of empty spaces as the headlights lit up their way. "Lord, it's so empty here. Nothing at all. Not a farm, not a house. So desolate . . . but I like it. Sort of like riding along a road on the moon," She wiggled back against the soft leather. "And I'm certainly glad you know the roads up here on the moon."

"There's only one way to go. You drive out of Malafortuna, up the mountain twenty kilometers, and you're at the lookout. It's just about midway. Then down the mountain twenty kilometers and you're in Torriano. That's all there is."

"The lookout? Is that the place 'way up where you can pull over and see for miles over the mountains with all of Malafortuna below you?"

That's the place. You can see the road corkscrew around the mountain below you. If you look straight down, you can watch anyone who drives up. The lookout's where all the kids in both villages come to kiss and snuggle."

"Ah," said Julie inadequately as the car came to the lookout. Alessandro slowed the car for a moment and Julie felt her heart slide around in her chest. For an instant, she thought he might stop and the idea of being there, alone on top of the world with Alessandro beside her, made her heart stop its slide and begin to pound against her skin. Involuntarily, she put her hand up to keep the sound inside her chest. She felt hot, then sweaty, then ice-cold. She looked outside, trying to keep herself from behaving like a love-sick fool in front of him. The headlights lit up the rocks piled against the edge of the drop-off and swept around the parking area. She could see a dark colored car parked over by the edge, near a stand of bushes. In the quick light, she could see no heads visible above the seats. *They must be making out*, Julie thought and the flush of heat on her chest and neck was instantaneous. Alessandro laughed and blew the horn to jolt the lovers. They laughed, but their laughter was strained as each thought of being there with their arms around one another, close in the darkness of their car, so alone up here under the stars. The Ferrari completed the turn and picked up speed as they drove down the crooked mountain road into Torriano. The pink slowly left her cheeks and her heartbeat stopped its crazy thump.

Under cover of the darkness, the heat left Alessandro's neck and ears. He'd never quite met anyone like her before. No one that had ever gotten under his skin like she had. He'd been unable to stop thinking about her all week, castigating himself for his stupid behavior on the night of the dance. She'd been right --he *had* acted like an asshole. His life *was* superficial and selfish. But who would have *dared* to say anything? His mother? His employees? No, no one. Before Julie, no one had ever criticized him for anything at all. His life had run along a charmed path, with everyone he knew standing on the sidelines cheering him on. It was true. He'd only received praise and adulation and he walked along the golden, flower-strewn path like a spoiled child.

He tried to think. When had anyone told him he was wrong about anything? When had anyone ever called him an idiot to his face? Certainly not anyone at his firm. Certainly not Kendra. No one, except perhaps Nonna

Caterina, once in a while. And maybe Mamma, if he looked deeply enough into her eyes. He bit his lip, feeling a tiny bit guilty. Even if there were a little bit of criticism, would he have felt obliged to listen to it? No. Not at all. Of course, there was his ex-wife. She'd done nothing *but* complain. Poor Renata. What a bad match they'd been. He remembered when she'd found his tiny slice of vulnerability, and then cut his heart out. He shook himself mentally and thought hard--who else had criticized him? Maybe Renzo, fifteen years ago. He remembered Renzo arguing with him, shoving him, threatening him. It had been about Carmella. She'd been like a ripe apricot in those days, sweet and juicy and Renzo had been nuts about her. The argument had started when Alessandro tried to take her away from his best friend. It had been a joke. Just a joke, except Renzo really was in love with her and hadn't thought the joke was funny at all. And Carmella hadn't wanted to go out with Alessandro anyway. Funny, he hadn't thought of that in years. He bit the inside of his lip. He'd been a jerk even then, and only Renzo, his blood brother, had told him so. He cringed with shame even now, thinking about what an idiot he'd been.

But after that, after he'd left Renzo and Malafortuna behind, all he'd ever heard was praise. How smart you are, Alessandro! How astute in business! How brilliant, starting your own company and becoming rich in only a few years! How well you run your corporation, Alessandro, grabbing every contract away from everyone else, no matter how ruthlessly. How marvelous you are! And handsome too! How well-dressed you are, Alessandro, and how fantastic you are in bed!

Julie's face had been in his imagination for six days now. He hadn't been able to get her out of his mind. In his imagination, she'd listened to every word he'd said and snickered at the glib falseness that poured out of his mouth. He never realized what complete bullshit passed for normality through every part of his day. He'd heard her laugh, mocking the posturing glamour, the empty pretentiousness of his life, and when he picked up Kendra for dinner, Julie's image sat at the extra chair, rolling her grey eyes at the superficiality of their chatter.

And she'd been perched at the end of Kendra's bed, laughing at him as he whispered the same stale words that he mouthed to every woman he seduced so easily. And when he gasped in the throes of the mechanical sex he performed, she watched him silently and he saw that her eyes were filled with tears.

"A penny for them," she spoke now and his foot nearly slipped off the clutch as he jerked himself back to the reality of the night.

"A what?"

"I suppose I should say a *lira*. In America, when the person you're with hasn't said anything for a while, you offer them a penny for their thoughts. I guess it means, 'what are you thinking of now'?"

"I'm thinking of you," he said, disconcerted by his mind's fancies. He took one hand off the steering wheel and touched the top of her hand for a moment. "I thought about you all week."

"You did?" She smiled in the darkness, pleased beyond belief. She had certainly thought about him. He'd been with her all week. She'd talked to him when she kneaded bread, having imaginary conversations where he told her how much he loved her and she told him that she loved him too. She'd whispered his name into her pillow at night, wondering if his lips would taste like she thought they would and wondering what she would do if he really kissed her. The car glided to a stop and she was astonished to find they were in Torriano, on a narrow dark street in front of a dimly lit door with a bent and battered sign that said "Luisa's".

"*Andiamo*," he said, turning off the engine and stretching. Her mouth went dry at the sight of his body flexed in the leather seat. He didn't seem to notice and she shivered as he got out of the car. He opened her car door and took her hand to help her out. "I hope you enjoy this as much as I think you will."

The restaurant seemed filled with people, the clink of silver and glass and the smell of delicious food. A tiny woman, bent with age, screeched when she saw Alessandro at the door. She ran over and held her arms out for his embrace. He picked her up off the floor as if she were a child. "Alessandro! *Bello Mio!* You big ox! What a surprise! Why have you stayed away so long?" She hit his shoulder with her little fist and kissed him, smack on his lips. And then, seeing Julie, "And who is *this?*"

They sat in the garden, away from the crowd. Their wooden table was under a tree that smelled like oranges and Luisa fussed over them herself, all the while keeping up a stream of talk berating Alessandro for being away for so long. "Nevermind that you order. I will bring you the best." She bustled out and brought back glasses of rough red wine and a dish of cracked olives. A smiling ten-year old boy put a basket of hot bread on the table. It was new-baked and came with a dish of fresh butter with chopped herbs on top.

"He's Luisa's grandson," Alessandro explained, his mouth full of bread.

Luisa popped back with a platter of *papardelli*, ribbons of pasta covered with a sauce of fresh, earthy mushrooms. *Not 'napped', with the sauce in a decorative puddle with a dimwitted sprinkling of parsley as a design around the lip of the bowl*, Julie thought happily, *but lavishly ladled over*. They hungrily mopped up the sauce from the bottom of the dish with the rest of the bread, licking their fingers and grinning like two urchins.

The old lady beamed while they ate, holding her two claw-like hands under her chin, and then she brought them a platter with pork cutlets cooked with fresh figs and a syrupy red wine. It defied description and Julie closed her eyes in ecstasy. "You like?" Julie nodded joyfully. The grandson brought over *espresso* in tiny blue cups and two glasses of *sambucca nero, "con mosca,"* Luisa said, dropping three coffee beans into Julie's glass. "It means with flies in it - see? The coffee beans look like flies, no? And it's good luck to have three beans. One for each. The Father, The Son and The Holy Ghost!" Her wrinkled cheeks chuckled at the confusion on Julie's face. "I know it doesn't make much sense, but that's how we do it," and she gave Julie three more coffee beans. "Now you do it for Alessandro." She held Julie's hand in her claw for a moment and told her that if the beans sank to the bottom of the glass, it meant that he and Julie would be friends, but that if they floated on top of the *sambucca*, they'd be wed within a year.

Julie's eyes looked unflinchingly into Alessandro's. She dropped the beans, one, two, and three into his glass. "Eeeeee!" crowed Luisa as the beans floated gently on top of the dark liquid. Julie blushed furiously and Alessandro felt a bursting in his soul. He picked up Luisa's hand and kissed it. Luisa batted him on his shoulder and held up one finger. Her grandson put a small platter in the middle of the table. "Three for each of you," she said, and left them alone.

There were six tiny cookies on the plate. Two were button-sized butter cookies that tasted of vanilla, two were crumbly rounds of pine nuts and the last two were fingers of chocolate and spice. Julie popped them, one by one, into her mouth. She had been treated to a meal of simple, absolute, perfection. This, *this* was what she was searching for! *This* was sublime!

Only after Julie promised that she'd be back in the next few weeks to watch Luisa and help her in the kitchen did the old lady let them go. "Have a good time at the dance," she ordered. "And be nice to your ladyfriend." She nudged Alessandro in the ribs sharply. "Don't let this one get away. She's too good for an ox like you."

They walked to the square and their hands brushed and they bumped a little into one another. Each time she touched him, Julie felt a tiny flame leap from her hand or her hip. She tried to see if Alessandro had any reaction, but his face was impassive and she couldn't tell what he was feeling.

He told her without being asked. "God, I'm full!"

That's what you get, Julie, my girl, she admonished herself. "Me too. That was the best food I've ever had. Just right. Perfect."

"Even in the company of an asshole?" He asked gently.

She ducked her head. "Even that."

They turned the corner and saw the lights from the square. Renzo's band was already playing and the music floated out over them. Julie clapped her hands. "It's like Malafortuna, but bigger."

"And noisier." He took her hand and led her through the crowd, nodding to a few people here and there. Renzo saw them and pointed to a table near the front.

"So, my old friend," he sat down with them as the song ended, "How did you head feel last week, eh?"

Alessandro made a face. "It still hurts, Renzo. You saved me, though, blood brother. If you hadn't dragged my home, I'd still be there."

"Blood brother?" Julie asked and they told her stories about when they were young, laughing and pounding one another on the shoulders. Julie's eyes danced as she saw a glimpse of the Alessandro who had been a carefree boy so many years ago.

"Remember the goat?" Renzo asked.

"The goat! That was the best ever!" And the two of them roared while Julie watched. Before she could ask why they laughed so hard, Renzo saw one of the band beckoning to him. The second set of the night started and Renzo groaned as he got up to play. The first song was "Mala Femina", and Alessandro pulled Julie gently up and into his arms. He closed his eyes and sighed, pressing his jaw against her coppery hair.

It was late as they drove up over the mountains and Alessandro held her hand the whole way. She was in a daze, scarcely letting herself think and when they reached the lookout, her heart stopped beating. He told her, "It is a rule. We must stop." She could hear the tension in his voice as he tried to keep the moment light. He'd been waiting all night for this.

She wet her lips with the tip of her tongue. "Yes. I think we should." Her words were steady, belying the beat of her heart. "Just for a moment," her voice dropped to a whisper. She ached for him.

"These two must be going for the endurance record," Alessandro said as he noticed that the dark blue car was still parked in the same spot. Julie stiffened slightly. Why did that damn car still have to be here? It . . . It . . . Well, it *spoiled* the moment. She wanted to think that she and Alessandro were special, not just one of dozens of cars whose occupants were up here necking. Damn them anyway. And then Alessandro reached for her and all thoughts of the blue car flew out of her mind.

His hands held her jaw, imprisoning her face and he searched her eyes, asking her without words, and she answered him. He kissed her softly, with his eyes wide open, once on each corner of her lips and then he cradled her head gently and kissed her full on her mouth.

The touch jolted him. Her lips were like honey, too sweet to be borne, and he drowned in her taste and the heat of her mouth like an adolescent boy on his first date. She whispered his name and pulled him closer.

He, who had seduced so many women, couldn't think, couldn't breathe and he felt molten desire engulf him. There was a growling sound and then he realized it was coming from his soul. He felt like a primitive man, wanting nothing but this woman in his arms. His body was on fire. He ached for her and when his kiss deepened and she pulled his tongue inside her mouth, he leaped convulsively. His hands molded the sides of her breasts and she arched her body into him. He bent her backwards, trying to touch as much of her as he could, but the inside of a Ferrari wasn't made for comfortable love. "Julie . . . *Carissima*," he gasped and then his hand slid on the softness of her leg, high and higher. She splayed her hand against his chest, unable to think or breathe and then her breath sucked in as he touched her and then she cried out.

His breathing was harsh and he held her away from him for a moment. He closed his eyes and groaned in passion. "Ah, Julie. . . . " Her face was hot and flushed and her eyes were glazed with desire. "This damned car. . . . " he swore. "There's no room to move." She gulped thickly, trying to quiet the thud of her heart and then they both began to laugh at the absurdity of their plight.

"I'm a tall girl," she said ruefully. "I take up a lot of room."

He kissed the tip of her nose, giving himself time to compose his raging need. "Let's get out of the car." His eyes gleamed and he worked his eyebrows up and down, like some American vaudeville comic and then his face sobered. "I never wanted anyone like I want you, *Cara*. Never."

She nodded, unable to even smile. "This is madness," she said as she opened her car door wondering how far it would all go. A little voice in her head made fun of her. *You know how far it will go, Julie, sweetie-pie. All the way to the end of the road, darling. All the way up and back down again.*

He got out of the car and they stood together, hands linked loosely. They could see the few bright pinpoints of light that were Malafortuna in the distance of the nighttime. The cool mountain air blew across her hot face and she thought about what might come next. *Did she really want to do this? Yes! Yes,* screamed her heart and she turned to him. He took her into his arms. She could feel his heart thudding through the jacket he wore. He pushed her gently back against the car, bending her back slightly and then pressing his full weight against her body. He was heavy and solid and she could feel the hardness of his desire as her body curved to meet him. *I wonder what we'll do about condoms,* she thought. *I never thought to bring any. I don't think I have any to bring. I guess he'll have one and I suppose now I'll have to go and get some.* And then his lips came down and he kissed her hard, lingeringly, his mouth devouring hers. She collapsed against him and there was no room for any coherent thought in her brain.

His legs spread open slightly to support his weight and she was pinned between them. One of his hands moved down, following the curve of her hip, and he caressed her, his thumb on the bone of her hip socket and his fingers molded to her back. He bent his head further and began to nibble on her neck and the soft skin of her collarbone. She held his head and kissed the top of his dark hair. She closed her eyes, the better to savor the sensation of his mouth on her. She shifted slightly and opened her eyes. Something . . . Something was intruding. "Alessandro," she said and he groaned and brought his hand to the side of her breast. His lips nipped at the hollow of her neck and his thumb moved to her nipple. She ached with want and sucked in her breath, drowning in the feel of him. She was on fire. She wanted him and wanted his touch everywhere. Her hand slid down his body and he whispered to her. She bit at his earlobe and then, out of the corner of her eye, she saw the blue car.

"Not here," she whispered urgently. "Not with these other people around." And she pushed him away slightly.

He swore. Some dialect Italian words that she had never heard before and he raised his fist toward the blue car.

"Alessandro?" Her voice was odd. "That car was here when we came before we had dinner. That was hours and *hours* ago. Why is it still here?"

"I don't know. I don't care. Darling, listen to me . . . " he urged her with his lips.

"No. Wait. Something's not right. Maybe someone is sick or something."

"*Merde*," he said, realizing that the moment had passed.

"Let's see if anything is wrong." She pulled him towards the other car and he shrugged, half-annoyed, as his ardor cooled. It just wasn't to be, that's all. For some reason, God was metering out some punishment to him for all the bad things he'd ever done.

"Wait. Let me get a flashlight. If I can't make love to you, at least we ought to see what the hell we're doing." He rummaged in the trunk of his car and then switched on the powerful beam. She bit her lip, hopping from foot to foot, thinking that she'd made an awful fool of herself.

The blue car was a Cortina. It looked deserted and they gingerly approached the driver's side. Alessandro trained the flashlight on the interior of the car. What was *that*? He peered hard through the windshield, trying to see inside. Ugh! He tripped hard and nearly fell over and then, trying to see what made him stumble, tipped the flashlight's beam down.

"Ahhhhhhhh!" Julie grabbed him hard and her scream echoed in the night, echoing off the mountaintops. "Oh, My God! Oh, My God!" She gasped and they both saw the dead woman's face in the flashlight beam.

"She's dead!" Julie's arms wound around him and she cried out. Alessandro's throat gagged at the dark splotches that could only be blood. His eyes gaped at the hacked and butchered body. He turned away, retching and Julie took the flashlight from his nerveless hands and played it up and down on the woman's bloodied torso. "Jesus!" She gasped. "Oh, dear, sweet Jesus!"

He wiped the bile on his sleeve and clutched her arm. "Let's get the hell out of here."

"Wait! We can't just leave her here like this!" Julie waved the flashlight around, lighting up the bushes. "What do you think happened?"

"She was *killed*, Julie! What the hell do you think happened! *Gesu e Maria!* We can't stay here. Suppose the killer is still around?" Her eyes were huge and she began to shake. He took the flashlight from her. He circled her waist with his arm and held her behind him, protecting her from any assailant who might be lurking. "Stay still. Don't move. I'm going to look around." He flashed the light around and then aimed the light into the window of the car. "Holy Mother of God!" His voice was quivery. "There's a dead *man* in the car."

"*What!*" she cried out. Her eyes goggled as she looked through the glass. Before she could think, she wrenched the door of the car open. Slowly, framed in the beam of the flashlight, the body of a man, his face as bloody as the woman's, toppled out. The man's body crumpled in a heap at their feet, with his head resting on the tip of Julie's shoe. She made a funny noise and fainted into Alessandro's arms.

"Julie! Julie!" He dropped the flashlight and it bounced on the ground, landing near the man's torso. He held Julie in his arms, for a moment thinking that she, too, had died. His heart stood still and then she moaned and he shook her hard. She opened her eyes, and his face swam in front of her.

"Are they really dead?" she whispered fearfully and he nodded his head, holding her against him as if he would never let her go.

CHAPTER SEVEN

They argued fiercely for several minutes over who would stay and who would go to get the police, their voices harsh whispers over the stares of the dead faces. In the end, only Alessandro could safely drive on the narrow ribbons of road that wound down to Massimo's house. He gave her the flashlight and kissed her hard. She could hear him say something unintelligible as he leapt into his car and drove away.

It was scary. She was left in the darkness with only the flashlight to keep her fright at bay. Dismally, she watched the Ferrari's tiny red taillights weaving in and out of the mountains until they disappeared from view. It should take him fifteen or twenty minutes to drive to Malafortuna, say ten minutes to wake up Massimo and explain what they had found, and perhaps another twenty minutes for them to return. She shivered and wondered if the batteries would last that long. She didn't think she could just sit here in the dark without losing her mind.

Experimentally, she shut off the flashlight. It was inky black and the hairs on her arms stood up straight. Frightened, she switched the beam back on and felt silly for her fears. *There's no one here*, she told herself fiercely. *No one except those two dead people.* She shut the switch off again, to save the batteries. Just in case she really needed them. She tried to think of something –anything but the two people laying there—murdered by some butchering lunatic. She thought about Alessandro and how much she was attracted to him. She focussed on the evening, remembering every item on Luisa's table, went over their dinner, course by course and then tried to remember the names of the songs that Renzo had played. She thought about Alessandro's face and the way his nose looked. A little smile curled her mouth. He'd been lovely all night. There hadn't been one single hint of the annoying man from last week. Could she love him? She swallowed thickly and thought of where the night would have led had it not been for their grisly discovery. She would have let him make love to her. Definitely. She rocked back and forth. Was it a good thing that they had stopped? Would he have thought her an easy woman if she'd capitulated?

There was a crackling noise in the bushes. Her hair stood back up on end. "Who's there?" she said loudly, into the night. "Jack! Bring the flashlight here! There's someone in the bushes!" She snapped on the flashlight and tried to talk in a deep voice. Hopefully, whoever it was would think that there was a man with her, and perhaps they'd be afraid of Jack. The night was quiet now and she played the beam of the light over the bushes to total silence. *Probably an animal*, she prayed. She walked gingerly over toward the Cortina. The bodies were still sprawled exactly where they had been. Her breath whooshed out. She certainly had the heebie-jeebies! Well, who could blame her?

In another moment or two she was bored stiff. *How can I be terrified out of my mind and bored at the same time*, she asked herself? She inched closer to the woman's body. *I wonder who she is? Hmmmm. She looks nice, I mean if she wasn't dead. About fifty, a little overweight with brown hair and one brown eye, anyway.* The other eye was battered closed. Funny, but the body didn't seem quite so awful as it did a half hour ago. She shook her head. *I can't believe I'm almost comfortable with them now, the two poor souls.* She played the flashlight up and down their bodies. They've been dead for a long time now, she noted. The blood was all dried and in the beam of the light it looked like black ribbons and splotches where it had flowed and puddled. Julie wasn't very religious, but she said a prayer to God to help her catch whoever had done this to these people.

After a few more minutes, she squatted and peered at the clothes the woman wore. A blue-flowered blouse and a light blue skirt. They looked American, somehow. Sort of house-wifey. *Talbot's*, she thought, *not the Via Veneto*. She aimed the beam at the woman's feet. Unbidden, words came to her and she sang: "One shoe off and one shoe on . . . deedle, deedle dumpling, my son John." *I'm losing my mind*, she goggled. *Going stark raving mad! Singing nursery rhymes at a time like this*! She poked at the shoe lying on its side and felt a glow at her brilliant deducting. Size 7 1/2 M, Naturalizers. Bingo. The woman was definitely an American.

Unabashedly nosy now, she went over to the man. He looked about sixty, had a conservative haircut and wore a blue and white striped shirt and dark blue slacks. His shirt looked American, too. Italian men's shirts were more tapered and usually made from silk or linen. This was 100% polyester cotton or she'd eat her hat. She stepped over the man and stuck her head into the car. She'd seen enough detective stories on TV to know about preserving the scene of the crime. She'd be careful not to touch anything, but she was suddenly very, very curious.

There was no handbag, no luggage and no papers of any kind. Only the woman's suit jacket, the same light blue material as her skirt. Julie aimed the flashlight on the jacket and then jumped back as if she'd been stung. *Fancy's?* The label said "Fancy's"? How could that be? She looked again and then said, "I'll be damned!" out loud.

Fancy's! Who could believe that she'd be so far from home, stranded on a hillside in Italy in the middle of the night. Who could think that she might meet a man like Alessandro, stop on a mountain to make love, and then stumble over two dead bodies-- and that one of them would be wearing a suit from Fancy's Emporium! Fancy's! On Greenwich Avenue! In the US of A! Fancy's! The dress shop she and her parents and her grandparents had been buying clothes from ever since the Sabatinos and the Fioriles had come to America! Who could believe it! She looked at the woman with a new interest. A personal interest. The woman must be from Connecticut!

Jubilant now, and almost at home with her corpses, neighbors from home, Julie poked and pried all over the car. There must be some clues! She felt like Nancy Drew, trying to be careful and not leave fingerprints. But there was nothing else that she could see. The glove compartment was empty and there was nothing under the seats. Nothing tucked down under the cushions. Nothing on the floor. "Rats!" she moaned and then remembered the trunk.

It was locked. She bit her lip and thought, then tried an old trick to open the trunk, using the edge of the flashlight. Her brother Moe had taught her how to jimmy trunks open when they had been teenagers. "Moe, baby. Help me now," she pleaded with him, even though he was halfway around the world. The trunk popped open and she yelled, "Yippee!" into the night air.

The trunk held a spare tire, a jack and a yellow plastic bag that contained a flashlight, jumper cables and a tool set. Disgusted, she slammed the lid down, and then, remembering something, opened it again. The yellow plastic bag was lettered on the outside. "*AltoViso Noleggio Macchine, Roma*". Ha! The car was a rental. From AltoVista Car Rental. Rome. Bingo again!

She closed the trunk again and went back to the woman, feeling as if they were friends now. After all, they shopped in the same store, didn't they? She knelt down next to the battered face. "I'm going to find out who did this to you," she solemnly assured the corpse. "I won't let you down." She patted the body on its arm and nodded, almost as if she were talking with her. She leaned over, trying to see something more, so intent on making contact, somehow, with the essence of this lady, that she didn't hear the roar of the engines until the beams from two cars flashed across the mountain just below her.

Hurrying, before they came, she looked again for anything --*anything*-- that might help. Nothing, really, except that there was an angry red mark on the woman's neck and a band of white skin, coupled with a swollen knuckle on the woman's left ring finger. Julie thought that the killer had probably pulled off the woman's wedding ring. "Why do I think she was married?" Julie asked the night. "She just looks married," she told herself, still speaking out loud to keep to herself company. "And was there more than one killer?" she asked herself. "Hard to be sure," she muttered the answer and then the headlights swept onto the lookout and she was wrapped tightly in Alessandro's strong arms.

Massimo got out of the second car. He was wearing his regulation police pants and a striped pajama top. His hair, usually groomed to mimic the latest male model on the cover of *"Oggi"* Magazine, was in wild disarray. "*Merde!* Alessandro, You weren't kidding!" He whistled as he inspected the murder scene.

"Hey! Help me out." He handed Julie and Alessandro an end of the special yellow tape that was used to rope off crime scenes. They set up flares and cordoned off the area of the blue car and the two bodies. In the glare of the red flames of the flares, it looked like a scene from Hell.

Massimo rubbed his hand over his chin, "Hmmmm. They're dead all right."

He'd been a policeman for nearly eighteen years. His Zio Beppo had put his application on top of the pile when Old Orazio, who had been town policeman since Caesar's Legions had tromped all over Malafortuna, died. It was easy for Zio Beppo to get Massimo the job. Zio Beppo had connections. And no one else wanted it.

Massimo had been surprised that no one else wanted the job. It was a good job, paying more than enough money to a man who still lived at home with his mother. And the Italian patronage system insured that anyone who held the job for twenty-five years would get a decent *pensione* for life. And besides, the job gave him two new uniforms a year and a hat. And paid for the *benzina* for his car and the two decals which showed the seal of the Italian Government. Massimo was of the opinion that the government should have supplied him with a car as well, but, well, he could always pad his mileage a little, couldn't he?

It was the opinion of everyone that Massimo Nulla had been born lazy. He was three weeks late and his mother had to drink a quart of castor oil in order to induce him out of her womb and into the world. She'd loved him wildly. Perhaps that was because Massimo's father wasn't the man that Massimo's mother was married to. No. No. Although no one but his mother knew, and she would carry this secret to the grave, Massimo's father was an actor from Assisi who had come with the opera company one summer.

They'd only been married three months, Massimo's mother and her husband. On the night of the opera performance, both of them had too much wine to drink. The man Massimo's mother was married to fell asleep halfway through the first aria, and she left him there, snoring in his seat. On the way out, the actor from Assisi saw her. He invited her backstage to see the opera from a better vantage point. Nine months and three weeks later, Massimo was born. The man Massimo's mother was married to rejoiced that he had such a strong and handsome son. Two years later, on the very day that he was due, Massimo's mother gave birth to Renzo. Both boys were handsome, with dark, curly hair and brilliant smiles. But Massimo was always his mother's favorite. Two years after that, the man Massimo's mother was married to died working on the railroad, and Mamma Nulla was left with his railroad *pensione* to bring up her two sons with the help of *her* mother, Nonna Graziella.

The two Nulla boys looked very much alike. Temperamentally, though, they were very different. Massimo was said to be lazy, easy tempered, good natured, happy to live at home with his Mamma and Nonna. Renzo was industrious, a hard worker with a quick temper and a readiness to jump into any fight. Renzo could make music from a tree branch, hated school and could always be found making mischief with his best friend, Alessandro Alessi. He hated living at home and would often be found sleeping in Zio Nunzio's haystack instead of his own bed. Mamma Nulla was very happy when Renzo married Carmella DeCarlo and moved into the second floor of the DeCarlo house. She loved each and every one of her four grandchildren, and knew she would adore the new baby that would be here in three months, but she still loved Massimo better than anyone else.

Being Malafortuna's policeman was the perfect job for Massimo. There wasn't a great deal of crime in Malafortuna or the neighboring towns. Whether that was due to nature, or to the fact that Massimo was, indeed, a good policeman, know one could say. And what crime there was, he took care of right away. A little robbery. A few sheep stolen at one time or another. A couple of drunken brawls. Children's mischief, petty things, and Massimo kept on top of it all and still had plenty of time to go out with girls and sleep under the grape arbor. Few could see beneath Massimo's mantle of indolence and see the orderly mind below. In truth, Massimo loved the law and he was proud that he kept his little village free of crime and disorder.

For instance, take the robbery of Signora Ventura's golden cross. Easily solved when her drunken lout of a husband tried to pay for the third bottle of wine by pawning the cross in Torriano. And the missing sheep? Ah, the culprits were located easily when the men of Saint Sofia Social Club celebrated their twelfth anniversary with a lamb supper for fifty people and Massimo bought a ticket. The entire membership donated two thousand *lire* each and the farmer whose flocks had been raided was soothed with a bundle of money.

Certainly, keeping the peace in Malafortuna was simple. Except for this. *This* was beyond belief!

They waited on top of the mountain until Elio Nargi, the Chief of Police of Torriano, and technically, Massimo's superior, made his way to the lookout. The car disgorged Nargi, two men who dusted everything for prints and evidence, a photographer and two more policemen. Julie thought they looked like one of those little teeny cars at the circus that dozens of clowns keep coming out of.

Nargi was a short, stringy man with a sharp nose, eyes set rather too close together and a sharp manner. He treated Massimo with contempt. "Stand over there, Nulla, and keep your hands to yourself. Try not to get in our way. This is obviously a robbery and I'll be handling it." Massimo opened his mouth to speak and the Chief yelled at him to be quiet.

Julie and Alessandro sat on the rocks with Massimo and watched the men crawling around. Julie whispered that she didn't like the Chief at all, and wasn't that too bad because she had an important clue that no one else would ever discover. Nargi heard her whispering and asked her in an acid tone if she would mind keeping quiet while his men were working. Alessandro's eyes smoldered and he almost jumped up to confront the Chief, but both Julie and Massimo held him back.

In a half-hour the Chief came back to where they were sitting. "You can go home now," he glared at them, "We won't need you any more here tonight." His sneer turned to Massimo; "It's good luck for you that you didn't mess around with the crime scene, Nulla. God knows what your fat hands might have destroyed." Massimo started to speak again but Nargi put up his hand and began to walk away. Julie stuck her tongue out at his departing back. The Chief stopped suddenly and whirled around, almost as if he had eyes in the back of his head. Julie's eyes widened as he came back to them. "Be sure to be ready tomorrow to be questioned by my men," his voice was almost insolent. "We will be confirming your story about being in Torriano until midnight."

"What a shithead!" Julie boiled as they got into their cars.
Massimo smiled sweetly at her and told her not to think about anything at all until tomorrow. He winked at her and said, "He *is* a shithead." He got into his car and followed Alessandro's taillights down the mountain. He wondered if Chief Nargi had ever known anyone like Umberto and Vincenza Talerico.

Umberto Talerico had come from a small village across the mountains to marry Vincenza D'Ambrozio and to take over her father's prosperous farm. As a marriage gift, Umberto had given his bride a heavy gold necklace. Umberto was a hard worker, a decent husband, when he was sober, but every six months or so, he'd go on a bender that would last several days, coming home only when he ran out of money. It was the same every time. He'd rummage in his wife's underwear drawer, looking for enough cash to get him one more bottle of wine. And then, when he couldn't find any money, he'd rip the gold chain off Vincenza's neck and pawn it for the few coins needed to get another bottle. Vincenza would then come to Massimo, crying and cursing and swear that she was going to have her no-good husband arrested. The next day, naturally, Umberto would come crawling home, begging for forgiveness and swearing that it would never happen again. Stupid woman, she would wind up back in her husband's remorseful arms. She'd then take some money out of the top of her stocking and go to the pawnbrokers to redeem the necklace. Then, she'd come to Massimo, with triumph in her eye, and withdraw all the charges she had made against Umberto. There wasn't much Massimo could do about it but rejoice that he was still unmarried. It happened a few times every year. And the reason Massimo wondered if the Chief knew anyone like the Talericos was that every time Umberto ripped off the gold necklace, it left an angry red mark on Vincenza's neck. A mark exactly like the mark on the dead woman's neck.

On the way back down the mountain, Julie bounced up and down on the seat, telling Alessandro about the jacket label. "You see? No one but me knows where she's from!"

He looked at her in a worried way. "The police will get their names and address from the rental company. You keep out of this, Julie. There's a dangerous killer out there and I don't want you out there playing detective." His eyes went back to the road and he missed seeing the way her lower lip jutted out. If Alessandro had known anyone in Julie's family, they'd have told him that when she stuck her lip out like that, it meant trouble. But, as of this moment, Alessandro didn't know any of Julie's family.

He took her silence for agreement and stopped the car outside of her house. The lights were blazing in Marina's apartment, and Alessandro figured the entire town already knew that there had been two people murdered at the lookout. He sighed at the way his romantic evening had turned out. He put his arm around Julie and pulled her as close as he could. The Ferrari was the pride of his life, but it wasn't much of a car for romance. He saw his sister open the door and before she could come out, kissed Julie on the forehead. It was the best he could manage with most of the village peeking out of windows. "Put this all out of your head, Julie. Try to sleep well." He looked up, indeed, to see Marina's worried face at Julie's window and got out of the car to open Julie's door.

"It was quite an evening, Alessandro," she grinned at him. "You sure do show a girl a memorable time." She reached her arms around him and kissed him full and hard on his lips. Marina's mouth dropped open. The intensity of the kiss kept Alessandro awake for more than an hour after he went to bed.

✦✦✦

The Chief called Massimo early the next morning. Obviously, from the fawning note in his voice, the Chief had found out that Alessandro was the president of one of the biggest companies in Milano. "Why the hell didn't you tell me, Nulla?" he complained. "He's an important man!" Massimo shrugged. The Chief went on. "You bring them here and no excuses. I want to speak with them both. The American at eleven and Alessi at two."

"When is the autopsy?" Massimo had never been to an autopsy and when would he ever have another chance like this?

"Nevermind the autopsy." Nargi growled. "It's no concern of yours. Just have the American at your office at eleven."

"Julie." said Massimo.

"What?"

"Her name is Julie. Julie Stanton."

"I don't care if her name is Anna Magnani. Have her in the office at eleven!"

"And Chief," Massimo tried to continue, "There's something you ought to . . . ." But the connection had been broken and he could only hear the high pitched whine of an empty line. Massimo sighed and went to find Julie.

✦ ✦ ✦

When he came down to breakfast, Alessandro found his mother, Nonna Caterina, and Zia Nina sitting at the table with Claudio Boccadoro, the postman. "Mafia," Claudio said knowingly to him, making a gesture to show secrecy. Alessandro once again marveled at the speed that news found its way through the mountains. "It was them." Claudio put his finger to his head and pulled the imaginary trigger.

"There was no gun, bonehead," Mamma said disparagingly. "The Mafia would use a gun. This was a robbery, pure and simple. No money left, nothing in the car." She looked around triumphantly. Nonna was nodding grudgingly, but Zia looked doubtful. Claudio shrugged and made an elaborate face that somehow conveyed that he, as an employee of the Italian Postal Service, knew something more, but wasn't at liberty to tell. Mamma absently poured Alessandro some coffee and sat down, elbows on the table, waiting for him to tell them everything,

He took a big sip of coffee. "We stopped for a moment to see the view from the lookout . . . ," he started. They all hung on his words and for once, Nonna Caterina was completely speechless. The telephone rang in the middle of his recitation. It was Massimo asking him to be available at two o'clock.

"I think he'd like to pin the whole thing on you, me and Julie," Massimo warned gloomily.

And then Alessandro's mobile phone rang. It was Signora LaMonica calling from the office. He derived a great deal of pleasure from telling her that he wouldn't be in the office for several days. "I discovered two dead bodies last night and therefore I'm one of the prime witnesses in the murder case here." He heard her gasp.

"A murder, Signor?" Her usually starchy voice was squeaky.

"Yes. I'm sure you can read about it in the papers. I presume the headlines will say, 'Murder In Malafortuna'."

"I will immediately send someone out to get the Malafortuna editions." Signora LaMonica seemed back in her stride. "Were you in any way injured, Signor?"

"No. Fortunately most of the action was over by the time we reached there. I can't talk about it any further until I've been interviewed by the police." He paused delicately, "Are there any messages, Signora?"

She rustled some papers. "Miss D'Amor called twice this morning. She seemed quite insistent that she speak with you the moment you came in." Signora LaMonica had never approved of Kendra D'Amor.

"Please call her back and tell her that I've been delayed for at least several days," he looked up to see four pair of eyes watching him and digesting every word he said. He got up from the table and walked towards the kitchen so that they wouldn't be able to listen. The eight eyes followed him. "I'll call her as soon as I'm able to. The police tell me that I must be here." The little white lie came smoothly. The last person he wanted to see now was Kendra.

"But Signor Alessi," Signora LaMonica interrupted, "What do you want me to do about the Betadini account? Your meeting is scheduled for this afternoon."

The Betadini meeting! How the hell could he have forgotten? The account could be worth millions! "Ah," he tried to think. All he could dredge up was Julie's face. "I'd forgotten about the appointment." He heard Signora LaMonica's swift, indrawn breath. How *could* he have forgotten? "Um, Salvatore can take care of it, He can go in my place. Give him the blue folder on the top of my desk-- it's marked--and patch me through to his extension. Thank you, Signora. I'll keep in touch with you, " and he could imagine her face, incredulous, as she buzzed Salvatore Giotopolous.

"Salvatore? . . . Yes, thank you, I'm fine . . . but it will take a few days here to get through all the red tape . . . Yes. Yes, it was . . . I need you to go to the Betadini meeting this afternoon . . . No, No, Salvatore, you'll just have to go in my place. Explain it to the Betadini people and make my excuses . . . Of course you can do it. I have every confidence in you . . . Certainly. All the information is in the blue folder on my desk. Good. No, you can handle all the details." He heard Salvatore's excited gasp. "You'll be fine, Salvatore. You've been pestering me for years to let you make some decisions, here's your chance . . . I know it means millions. I told you, I have every faith in you . . . It's nothing, my boy. You'll be able to handle it as well as I could . . . Of course. I'll call you tomorrow and I expect to hear that you've sewn everything up. Use your brain, Salvatore . . . Yes, and of course, you'll continue to handle the entire account in the future . . . Certainly. Goodbye."

He could imagine what was happening in the office. For twelve years, ever since he started the company, he had never allowed anyone but himself to handle staggeringly huge financial deals like this one. And in a twinkling, he'd completely turned over the reins to his assistant. They must all think he'd lost his mind. He shrugged and the Betadini matter was forgotten.

He went back to the table. Claudio had taken himself, the rest of the mail and the gossip he'd gleaned to the next house and Nonna and Zia had gone out to the garden. Only Mamma was still in the kitchen and she threw out his cold coffee. "I'll make you a nice hot cup."

"Mamma?" She looked at him. "Do I act like a spoiled child?" She smiled as only a mother can smile, shrugged and nodded. "Do you ever feel like giving me a swift kick in the pants?" She nodded again, the smile still on her face, and put the coffee on the table. He added cream and three spoons of sugar. "Then why don't you?"

She stroked his cheek with the back of her hand. "Because you're a man, Alessandro. Not a little boy anymore." She kissed the top of his head. "And because I love you."

He took her hand and kissed the back of it. "Maybe you should kick me once in a while anyway, Mamma." He held the back of her hand against his cheek and closed his eyes for a moment, thinking about the two dead people. "And I love you too, Mamma." Sofia stood at the table, next to him, and blessed Saint Sofia for acting so quickly.

❖ ❖ ❖

She was ushered into the small dusty office in the Municipal Building marked "*Stazione Polizia*". Usually, anyone wanting to see Massimo on police business would find him at home, under the grape arbor, but this was a different kind of thing. The room was airless and Julie felt claustrophobic and nervous. Chief Nargi seated himself behind the desk. Massimo stood by the door, uncomfortably shifting from one foot to the other. There were two other policemen, one fat and one thin, sitting behind Nargi. The fat one had a notebook and pencil poised and the thin one was reading through a sheaf of papers.

"Sit down, Miss Stanton," Nargi waved his hand towards the chair pulled up in front of the desk. Julie considered saying that Stanton was her married name, but the expression on Nargi's face chilled her into silence. She perched on the chair, uneasy.

"Do you have your passport with you?" He held out his hand. She nodded and reached into her waistpack, handing him the folder with her identification. He glanced down briefly. "Giulietta Sabatino Stanton," he read and then looked at her expectantly. She nodded. Nargi turned to his fat compatriot. "Let the record state that the witness affirmed that her name is Giulietta Sabatino Stanton." The policeman wrote furiously and Julie mentally rolled her eyes.

"Why are you here?" he rapped out.

"Because you told me to come!". She was astonished at the question.

The Chief looked at her incredulously. "I presume you misunderstood me, Miss Stanton, and aren't being deliberately insulting." *Asshole*, she thought. *What a jerk*! She made sure that the expression on her face was respectful. "What I meant, Miss Stanton, is why are you here in Malafortuna? What brought you to a place so . . . so . . . bleak and desolate? So far from the comforts of America?"

"Oh!" She really wanted to scream out that she'd come here to murder two people on a remote hillside, but she doubted that he'd find any humor in such a remark. She nodded as if in grave understanding, "My great-grandfather came from here. His name was Salvatore Fiorile. I studied at a cooking school in America and graduated as a chef. I was seeking an unspoiled place to research Italian cooking."

"And so you came to Malafortuna?" his voice was sarcastic. Annoyed at him for denigrating Malafortuna, she nodded emphatically. "Please, Miss Stanton, you will have to answer with your voice."

"Excuse me. Yes, I came to Malafortuna.," she simply couldn't resist, "And I find it a wonderful place."

He watched her for a moment, then scratched his chin. "And tell me what you did yesterday. Everything."

In a pig's eye, she thought. "I woke up and had coffee with Marina Corbone, my landlady. She went off to work and I went back up to my apartment to type up the cooking notes from the day before. I worked until late morning and then went to La Famiglia for lunch at noon. I ate by myself, but I talked with Marco, the waiter and I was there for perhaps an hour." *Why does the officious little creep make me feel like a criminal*, she wondered. *Does he really think I killed those people?*

"After lunch, I went to Sopa's Bakery and helped Zara Pomafilla to make some cracked wheat bread." His curled lip told her what he thought of her consorting with those women at the bakery. "I left there about three in the afternoon and returned home. I washed my hair and got ready to go out for dinner with Alessandro Alessi." Nargi's eyes gleamed speculatively. "He picked me up and we drove over the mountain to Torriano. It was perhaps seven o'clock when we drove past the lookout." Uncontrollably, she blushed and Nargi's eyes widened slightly. "We, um, noticed that there was a dark blue car parked near the bushes. We didn't stop and it was dark. All we noticed was that the car was parked there. We arrived at Luisa's Ristorante, had dinner, walked to the square and spent the evening listening to Renzo Nulla's band." There was a squeak as Massimo's weight shifted and Nargi turned irritably toward him then looked back at Julie. "We left about midnight and began the drive home." She stopped.

"Go on. Go on." Nargi sounded impatient. The fat policeman stopped writing and the thin one stopped reading through his papers. They both watched her with smirks on their faces.

"We thought, um, that we'd, ah, stop for a few minutes at the lookout." Nargi's face was expressionless, but the thin policeman snickered. "We realized that the blue car was still parked in the same place and we became worried that perhaps someone was ill, or that the car was broken down." Her voice became smooth. It would be easy after the part about them stopping at the lookout. "Alessandro got a flashlight and we went over to the Cortina. He . . . Alessandro . . . stumbled over the woman's body and it was clear she was dead. We looked into the car and saw the man, and we knew he was dead, too. I opened the car door. I'm sorry that I touched . . . well . . . he fell . . . fell out of the car." her voice was flat. "Then Alessandro went for help."

"Did you touch anything else?" His tone was accusatory and she narrowed her eyes.

"The door handle. I'm sorry. That was all." Damned if she'd tell him that she prowled around in the car and jimmied open the trunk!

"Do you know who these people were?"

"Me?" Her voice was a squeak.

"Yes, you, Miss Stanton. Just answer the question." *Pompous little man*, she thought.

"No," she said truthfully. "I don't know who they were."

The Chief looked at two pieces of paper on the desk and made a few notations on a yellow pad. Julie sat, watching him. Her mouth was dry and she wanted in the worst way to scratch her nose. She wondered if she should tell him about the Fancy's label. "Let me give you some good advice, Miss Stanton." Nargi finally looked up at her. "You have already interfered with our crime scene. Please don't ever touch anything again when you find dead bodies." He was completely serious and she nodded, equally as serious. "That's all." He dismissed her with a wave of his hand. "We don't like foreigners here, Miss Stanton. You are lucky that I don't arrest you for making my job even harder. Please don't plan on leaving Malafortuna unless I give you permission. Do you understand?"

She nodded and then gulped, "Yes. Yes, I understand." She waited for a moment and when he didn't look up, stood up, nearly knocking over the chair in her nervousness. Massimo opened the door for her and gave her a tiny wink as she left the room.

Never! Never would she tell that pig of a man anything. Still, she felt frightened and ran down the steps and into the noonday sun. She stood for a moment, indecisive, and then headed for Zio Nunzio's farm and the cleanliness of the goats and chickens.

Alessandro's interview covered the same topics, although the Chief was careful not to be sarcastic in front of him nor chide nor warn him about anything. One never wanted to upset the Chairman of such a large corporation. In fact, Nargi nearly bowed as Alessandro left the room. "Thank you for your time, Signor Alessi." Massimo's eyes stayed fixed on the ceiling.

"The respect is mutual, Chief Nargi." Alessandro was faultlessly polite. "And may I know the names of the tourists?"

"The names?" The Chief repeated blankly. "Tourists?"

"Yes." Alessandro's eyes met Massimo's for an instant. "Massimo already brought it to your attention, didn't he? I'm sure that you noticed, as our capable local policeman did, that the people had rented from the car hire firm of *AltoVista* in Roma. I presumed you had already traced their names and addresses by this morning." Nargi blinked a few times and cleared his throat. The fat man started to speak and Nargi interrupted him roughly.

"The matter is under my control, Signor. Please be assured that the names will be available in a few hours." Nargi gave his men his sharpest glance.

"I would be pleased if you could let me know the names and addresses," Alessandro's voice was as smooth as the leather on the seats of his Ferrari. "I'd like to write to the families with my condolences."

"I will inform you as soon as the information is received," Nargi's voice was just as smooth as Alessandro's and the two men parted with handshakes.

"Why didn't you tell me about the rental firm?" Nargi hissed as soon as the door closed.

"I tried, Sir. I tried several times," Massimo was humble. "But you were always very busy and told me to keep quiet." His dark eyes were wide and innocent. "So, naturally, I presumed that you had noticed too."

The Chief's face was furious. "Of *course* I noticed, you village idiot. I can't imagine why we don't have that information yet. Get on the phone, Angelo," he snapped at the fat one. "Get the information right away!"

✦ ✦ ✦

Alessandro called Kendra from the privacy of his car. He told her about what had transpired. "I'm going to have to stay here for a few more days, Kendra. The police are insistent . . . I'm sorry about tomorrow night . . . No, there's no way I can be there . . . I understand, my dear. Please use the tickets. Take one of your girlfriends. Enjoy the performance . . . Of course, Kendra. Yes, I'll miss you . . . me too." The moment he hung up, she was out of his thoughts. He drove down the street to Marina's house and rushed up the stairs. "Julie? Julie!"

"Zio Alessandro?" His nephew was startled to see him.

"What are you doing here, Tonio? Where's Julie?"

"Please, Zio. I am called Anton now." The boy's voice held a note of pride. "I think Julie is at Zio Nunzio's farm. I am doing my homework."

"Anton? What a silly name." Alessandro spoke without thinking. "I thought you were supposed to be doing chores for Julie to make up for all the mischief you caused. Why aren't you working?"

With a peculiar look on his face, Anton had to explain. All about school.

And about wrecking Julie's terrace. About the deal Julie had made with him. And about the new name she had given him. His uncle followed every word and his own face showed clearly what he thought, changing as he listened to his nephew's tale or woe. First anger, amusement and then, finally, understanding.

"I never thought they'd hold me up to you like some tin god. I'm sorry Ton . . . Anton. It's not fair for you to be compared to me--or to anyone for that matter." He weighed the name and then, with his chiseled lips together, nodded thoughtfully, "Anton? A new name for a new start." He suddenly noticed what his nephew was wearing. "And a new pair of pants, too?" He started to laugh and Anton blushed painfully. "I recognize them. They're the ones I threw away last week because I ruined them."

"Nonna cleaned them and fixed them so that they'd fit me." The boy's face was red and he stammered, "I . . . She said they were too good to throw out."

Why I'm making the boy uncomfortable! Shit! I only meant to joke with him. Julie was right. I am a selfish idiot. Alessandro clapped his nephew on his shoulder and drew out a chair from the table. He sat down next to the boy and apologized. "I didn't mean to make fun of you, Anton. I'm just not used to dealing with you. The trousers look fine on you and I didn't realize how tall you're getting. Did Mamma have to hem them?" Anton shook his head. "No? Ah, Ton . . . Anton. Time goes so quickly and I never spend enough of it here." Anton looked at him in suspicious wonder, and Alessandro had the grace to blush himself. "You're right, my boy. I don't spend *any* of it here. Something I'm going to have to rectify." In discomfort, he fiddled with Anton's homework. He turned the paper around so that he could read it. "What are they teaching you in school nowadays?"

Amazed that his uncle showed any interest, Anton began to talk and Alessandro watched the young man who was such a stranger unfold before him. *He hasn't got it easy here*, Alessandro thought. *He's got the shadow of his father's desertion, Marina has no money to buy him decent clothes, and on top of it all, he's had to listen to his teachers rave about how smart I was. Poor kid.* He asked Anton a few more questions and the boy answered eagerly, his face lighting up. Alessandro felt a funny lump in the vicinity of his heart.

"And what do you want to do with your future?"

"I want to learn about automobiles," Anton's face was a beacon. "Perhaps go to work for you if you'll have me in your factory. I would do anything,

Zio. Even sweep the floor." And then the light went out of his eyes and he sighed.

"What's wrong? I'll give you a job when you get a little older, Anton."

"I couldn't leave Mamma," he said simply. His eyes lowered. "She will need me to help her here. Otherwise, she'd be alone."

Alessandro shifted on the chair. "Well," he said inadequately, feeling unaccustomed tears prickle, "We'll have to work out something. We need good apprentices in the factory, my boy. In fact, we can't get enough of young men who have the skills we need." He watched the light of hope flicker. "And now, I need some help to find Julie. Can you drive a car?"

"A car?" The boy shrugged bravely. "Sure."

"Good. Here are the keys. I want you to take my car to Zio Nunzio's farm." Anton's face was a study in confusion. His eyes asked the question and his uncle's eyes answered yes. His face grew incandescent. Did he really mean . . .? "Pick up Julie, if you'd be so kind. I'll wait here for the two of you."

"Me?" His voice was an incredulous squeak. "You want *me* to drive your Ferrari?"

"Please." Alessandro felt like singing out loud. "I'm too tired, Anton, my son. If you could go, I'd consider it a great favor."

CHAPTER EIGHT

Kendra D'Amor hung up the telephone distinctly annoyed. So what if he found a few murdered people? Why did that mean he had to stay in that god-forsaken fleapit in the mountains? She shrugged her ivory shoulders and allowed a frown to momentarily mar her perfect forehead. And she had bought such a gorgeous new outfit for the show! Her eyebrows rose up speculatively. She'd fix him, the big louse. She'd take the tickets and go anyway, dressed to make everyone notice her and the new man at her side, the good-looking new divorced gentleman who had moved to the third floor apartment. He'd been throwing glances and hints her way. Good! It would serve Alessandro right for leaving her on her own.

She tossed off her nightgown, leaving it on the floor for the maid to pick up. She stood, naked and perfect, studying her reflection in the long mirrored doors of her closet. She hefted the sculptured spheres of her breasts. The miniscule scars didn't show at all, even in the bright light of her dressing room. The doctor was worth his weight in gold. A tiny smile bent her mouth. She had certainly paid him his weight in gold, hadn't she? And a little more . . . how shall I say it? She made a kissing sound toward her reflection . . . a little more *personal* type of payment. She smiled widely and turned to the closet.

She chose a blue crepe dress and put it on, never tiring of watching as her reflection smoothed the material over her hips. Her eyes narrowed. Not quite right. She slid the dress off and left it in a puddle. Perhaps the green one? Yes. Perfect. She smiled generously at her reflection. She always looked perfect. It was her life.

She snapped on the television set and let the noise be a background to doing up her face. Almost automatically, she watched herself, noticing one tiny eyebrow hair out of place. She plucked it, then made sure that nothing, not even a hair, interfered with her loveliness. Perfection stared back at her. She was one of Milano's highest paid models and competition was waiting for the slightest sign of sagging, wrinkles or age. She did a little dance in front of herself. No one would push her off the top just yet. She scooped up the long fall of pale blonde hair that made men drool and women stare in envy and pinned it up into a towering chignon. A little spray and she was ready to go downstairs with the pair of tickets and a pleading look on her face.

Naturally, she hadn't been born with the classy name of Kendra D'Amor. Kendra D'Amor. She still smiled with satisfaction every time she heard it. She'd made up the name herself, and wasn't it the perfect name for her perfect face and body? Her mother and father had baptized her Concetta Piscatorra in a small church on the outskirts of Naples thirty . . . well, what did it matter how many years ago? She'd been the prettiest girl in the parish, with her long blonde hair, now artfully refreshed but who would ever know, and a pink and white complexion that made the nuns in the school watch her carefully with slitted eyes. She'd stood out like a beacon among her dumpy playmates. Kendra looked back scornfully at the days when every other child hated her and she couldn't wait for the chance to get away from the smells of peppers frying and her mother and father endlessly arguing.

One day, she'd taken some money from her mother's pocketbook and rode the train into Naples. Some of the money had bought her a black skirt, high stiletto heels and a black sweater. She'd thought about her name for a long time. Who would pay attention to anyone with such a rustic name as Concetta Piscatorra? No one. When the receptionist at the modeling agency asked her what her name was, she told her, Kendra D'Amor. "Go right in to the first booth, Miss D'Amor," the receptionist said, smiling mechanically. "Please change into the bathing suit that's hanging on the hook and someone will be with you in a jiffy."

Hers was like a fairy tale success story. Her figure and face had been her fortune and she'd used them in a businesslike, calculated way to get ahead. And now--everywhere in Italy--on posters, busses, magazine covers-- everywhere--soap labels, clothing, cosmetic advertisements--her face looked out from all of them, her lips pouty and bored, her hair artfully blowing in some unseen breeze. She was the one they wanted. And she intended to stay at the top of her profession, squashing down anyone who might try to to topple her off her pinnacle, until she married Alessandro Alessi and his fortune. Especially his fortune.

She had met him at a cocktail party nearly a year ago. "He's filthy rich and gorgeous!" Her friend had told her, "And I hear he's a stallion!" Kendra slid in and out among the people there until she reached Alessandro's side. She turned her dazzling smile at him and asked him if he'd get her a drink. In less than an hour, they were in bed together.

✦ ✦ ✦

Alessandro stayed for dinner at his sister's house because Julie was there. He wanted more than anything to be alone with her, to recapture the feelings from last night, but there didn't seem to be a moment when someone wasn't with them. Even as Marina put out a dish of marinated eggplant, Massimo Nulla strolled by. He wanted to talk about the murder.

"Sit down, Massimo," Marina smiled at him and swiftly added one more plate to the stack she held in her hands, "We were just about to eat." Alessandro sighed. Who else would crowd the kitchen?

Massimo sniffed the air and stuck his nose into the frying pan. "Mmmmm. *Giambotta*?" He poked a fork into the savory mixture of sautéed vegetables and picked out a piece of potato. "As good as my mother's," he said as he chewed it and then ducked out of the way of Marina's swat at his head.

"No woman alive will ever cook as well as your mother, Massimo. What girl would even try?" Massimo grinned, waggling his eyebrows, and speared another piece of potato.

Dinner was a cheerful affair with Anton bragging about how well he'd driven the Ferrari. The succulent *giambotta* half filled their plates and Marina paired it with fresh made hot pork sausages from Bruno Bastingliata, the butcher. Bruno made them from his secret recipe. Everyone in Malafortuna could make pork sausages, but somehow, Bruno's were better. The juices of the sausages mingled with the zucchini, eggplant and potatoes, and no one left a scrap on their plates, mopping up the sauce with chunks of Sopa's bread.

Julie contributed the dessert. "This was my Auntie Pierra's recipe, only she used apples instead of peaches." She had taken a few moments that afternoon at the bakery to make New England Peach Crumble from the last of Zio's peaches. The ladies at the bakery said that she could make a few when she came back in tomorrow, and perhaps they would sell them to the customers who might be looking for something new.

"Thank you, Julie. It was delicious," Anton's smile was dazzling and Marina smiled proudly at his new-found table manners. Heady with the success of his driving today, Anton stretched elaborately, "I'm going over to finish my homework with Chiara unless you want some help with the dishes." The adults watched him as he tried to walk casually away, and then they all burst into laughter.

"She's a sweet little girl." Marina said, watching the back of her son's head fondly.

"Her mother and Zara did a nice job bringing her up. They can be proud of her and she can be proud of them." Alessandro said, and then a strange look passed over his face.

"I didn't even know you knew Teodora or her daughter, much less Zara?" Marina's mouth fell open. "How do you know them?"

"How can I help know about them with Mamma and Nonna gossiping all the time?" Alessandro shifted uncomfortably on his chair.

Marina looked doubtfully at him and shrugged. "She *is* a nice little girl and Anton thinks she shines like a star. Now, all of you, shoo out on the terrace and you can talk about murder to your heart's content while I shut my innocent ears to the morbid talk and do the dishes." She made flapping motions with her hands.

"No thanks to Nargi's brain, they finally got the names of the two victims," Massimo told them, "Mr. and Mrs. Elgin Staney. Her name is Annabeth. " He stumbled over the unfamiliar "th" sound. . . . "And Elgin. What kind of a name is 'Elgin', Julie?"

"A silly one, Massimo. I think it's the name of a wrist watch."

"Anyway, he was sixty years old and she was fifty eight."

"Bingo!" Julie exulted. "I guessed their ages pretty well! Now for the big question. Where did they come from?"

Massimo fished into his top pocket and brought out a piece of paper. "Not from where you come from," he shook his head at her disappointed face. "No. They come from some place in New York . . . um, 23 Evergreen Drive, Port Chester, New York, USA."

He was smothered by her hug and whoop of joy. "*Port Chester!* Ha! I *am* the world's best girl detective. Port Chester is right next to Greenwich, just over the river."

"I thought you lived in Connecticut?" Massimo looked puzzled. The geography of America hadn't been one of his best subjects.

"Yes, but Greenwich is on one side of the river that bisects New York and Connecticut, and Port Chester is on the New York side. They're only a few miles apart." Massimo still looked puzzled. "Like if you live on one side of the mountains and on the other side is France." Julie's unusual explanation left him shaking his head as Julie sat back down with her chin cradled in her palm. "That's why she had on the blue suit from Fancy's store." She looked thoughtful. "Gosh, Massimo, she and I could have been shopping at the same time there!" Alessandro rolled his eyes heavenward. "Well, we might have been," Julie trailed off lamely.

"What were they doing here?" Massimo asked.

"Tourists?" Alessandro offered.

Together, Massimo and Julie chorused, "In Malafortuna?"

All three shook their heads in unison, "Nah."

"Then what were they doing here," Julie was puzzled. "*No one*, except someone like me trying to learn cooking would be stopping casually in Malafortuna." She colored slightly. "Not that I don't think it's a wonderful place."

"Maybe they got lost." Massimo shrugged. "They had rented the car for six weeks, so they intended to be in Italy for a while."

"Were there any fingerprints or clues in the car?" Julie was thinking furiously. "Anything at all to help us out?"

"Us? What's this 'us'? This is a grave matter for the police and Massimo, not for 'us'," Alessandro spoke sharply, seeing a vision of Julie's body covered with dark, dried blood. "You don't want to interfere with anyone who kills like that. This isn't some parlor game. Keep your pretty little nose in the oven where it belongs.

She opened her mouth to make a sharp retort. Quickly, before she could say anything, Massimo intervened, amicably waving his ham-fisted hands in the air. "Hey! No fighting over this! There's nothing more to know and if Nargi is running the investigation, that's all anyone will ever know." His mouth twisted. "The man is a empty-headed peacock." Julie reluctantly closed her mouth. Her face had a mulish expression on it. Who the hell did Alessandro think he was ordering her to stay in the kitchen? Julie caught Massimo's eye and he made a gesture with his head. They'd talk later.

The kitchen door banged and Marina came out, carrying a deck of cards. "We have to teach Julie how to play *Scopa*, no? She fanned out the deck.

"Now, you choose one card that will be the trump card." She shuffled the pack and offered it to Massimo. Julie joined in the game eagerly, but if someone were watching carefully, they'd notice that her bottom lip was sticking out. And if someone were watching Alessandro, they'd notice that he sighed resignedly. Cards! What other group activities would there be tonight?

Despite Julie's annoyance and despite Alessandro's desire to be alone, they all enjoyed themselves, playing *Scopa* and drinking wine, laughing at Julie's attempts to learn the intricacies of the game. Massimo played like a maniac, taking every opportunity to cheat outrageously and the evening flew by.

Alessandro was astounded at how late it was when Anton returned. "Are you all still here playing cards? It's after midnight!" He looked at his mother with teen-aged disapproval, and they all laughed uproariously and Anton didn't exactly know why. Midnight! How the hours had passed! Alessandro marveled. He'd only stayed to get an opportunity to be alone with Julie, dying to take her back in his arms and make her his own. Surprisingly, though, he'd enjoyed himself, with half his mind on the cards and the other half on her face. Now, she yawned hugely, stretching her arms up in the air.

"Goodness! I'm exhausted. I didn't realize it was so late." She gathered up the cards and stacked them neatly, handing them to Marina. "That was really fun. It reminded me of our all-night poker games when we were kids. I'll teach you all how to play American cards next time. And we'll play for money!" She stood up, managing to catch Massimo's eyes again. "I'm going to bed. Goodnight. See you all tomorrow." Massimo winked at her and she started up the stairs.

Alessandro leaped to his feet, nearly knocking over his chair. He almost ran to catch up with her. "Wait, Julie! I'll come up with you and say goodnight." His voice had the same offhand, casual sound that Anton's had held when he said that he was going to help Chiara with her homework. With nearly the same studied nonchalance, he followed her upstairs.

Anton went inside to go to bed and Marina began to pick up the wineglasses. "*Ciao*, Massimo," she bid him goodnight. "It was fun, no?"

"Are you sending me away so soon? Here," he took the glasses from her hands, "At least let me pretend to be of some help to you." He carried the glasses into the kitchen and put them into the sink. "You wash, I'll dry."

She started to protest, but then looked at him, holding her flowered *mopeen* in his big hands. She bit her lip, shrugged and ran the hot water.

Julie opened her door and turned to Alessandro. "Goodnight. It was a nice night, wasn't it?"

"Aren't you going to invite me in?" His voice was silky.

She looked at him, his face a dark shadow against the faint moonlight. He was the handsomest man she had ever seen and she wanted him with a fierceness she hadn't known she was capable of. She sighed and her face softened. Her lips parted. She reached up and put her hands on the sides of his face. She could feel the faint prickle of his beard and the palms of her hands tingled. She pulled his head down and heat spread through his body. She kissed his lips sweetly. "I'll dream about you, Alessandro," she said, making him dizzy. "And I'll see you tomorrow." And she was gone, leaving him standing with his hands halfway in the air.

She brushed her teeth in a trance. Had she done the right thing, or had she acted like some idiotic virgin? She'd be up half the night, tossing and turning and wishing he were next to her. She slid into the comfortable, well-worn sheets and thought about his face. The way his hair grew. In a moment, she was asleep.

In the morning sunshine, she awoke to the tail end of a dreadful dream. She'd been shopping at Fancy's Emporium with her cousin Carrie. She saw a blue dress and she tried to take it off the clothes rack. But someone else jerked the dress out of her hands. She turned to see who it was. She gasped . . . it was the woman in the car! Annabeth! She was pulling the dress away from Julie, trying to put it over her own head. And her head was battered and full of blood and when she tried to talk, blood poured out of her mouth. Her one good eye appealed to Julie, "Help me!"

Julie got out of bed slowly. There was no mistaking the message of her dream. She might be a modern girl, but she had been born a Sabatino. All the Sabatinos knew enough to believe in the power on their dreams. She washed and put on a shirt and some shorts as she calculated the time difference between Greenwich and Malafortuna. She slid on her sandals and went down for breakfast. "Do you mind if I use the phone before we eat?" She asked Marina. "I want to catch my brother Moe before he goes to work."

CHAPTER NINE

Moe Sabatino was an unusually happy man. Years ago, his great-grandfather Sal had left the starving village of Malafortuna, leaving behind a difficult childhood and the graves of his mother, father, young wife and baby daughter. There had been no reason to stay. The men on the ship with Sal told him incredible stories about America. There were golden streets where a man could merely stoop down to pick up riches. Sal was skeptical. Life hadn't been particularly good to him up 'til then and he was as hardheaded as any man who had come out of the mountains. When he reached America's shores, he saw that, in a way, the men had told the truth. There *was* gold to be picked up - the gold of opportunity. A chance curse and cuff at his head - "You wops are only good to pick up shit!" - made him understand where his own personal gold lay. With the last few dollars he had, Sal purchased himself two old mules, several long brushes, some shovels, some pails and a wagon. No one else wanted to do this kind of thing, and, in a few months, Sal had enough money to buy his own house. His new business, S. Fiorile - Garbage Pick Ups and Cess Pit Cleaning, was a roaring success.

It was three o'clock in the morning, early, with the whole day in front of him. The time Moe loved best. His easy, open face split into a grin as he greeted his dispatcher and opened the doors of the offices and garages. He was a handsome young man, strong, with curly red hair, a slightly darker shade than the copper tresses of his sister. Their grey eyes were nearly identical, definitely throwbacks to the Sabatino blood line and Francesca Sabatino Rosato, who had come to America in the early Nineteen-Hundreds with her brood of five children.

He whistled and sang a few snatches of some song, and, as he did every morning, made a huge pot of coffee for the twenty-seven men who worked for him, driving the huge blue and white Sabatino garbage trucks, the trucks that picked up refuse from nearly everyone in the affluent town of Greenwich. He'd finish his own route at eleven, wash up and scoot over to the factory where his steady girlfriend, Blanche worked. They'd walk down to town, have a hamburger lunch, and then the rest of the day was his. Man! He loved this business!

The coffee cup was hot in his hand as he swung himself up into the cab. Was that the telephone? Who the heck was calling him so early?

✦ ✦ ✦

"I *have* to see what I can do, Massimo," she explained earnestly. "That lady, Annabeth Stanley, she could have been a *friend* or a neighbor. We could have been standing back to back, choosing a dress or a blouse at the same time. I have to help find her murderer," Massimo nodded dubiously. "And then there was the dream," she went on. His eyebrows asked what was she talking about. "I dreamed that I was with my cousin Carrie, in Fancy's store." She looked at him as if that explained everything.

"Your cousin Carrie?"

"Naturally," she said. "There's no way that you could know this, but she went to Italy and helped solve a murder and break up a drug ring."

"Your cousin did this? Is she a policeman?"

"No," Julie laughed. "She just solved the crime and then *married* the policeman."[1]

Massimo scratched his chin. "Julie, I love you like a sister. I don't know what the hell you're talking about."

She looked at him pityingly, "So she was in the dream, see? That means *I* should try to solve the mystery, just like she did." And before he could object to this particular line of reasoning, she plowed on, "And then I was shopping and I saw the dead lady and she was trying to make me help her. Don't you see, Massimo?" She looked at him, praying that he would somehow understand.

He threw out his hands. "OK, Julie. Whatever you say." She was acting the way his Nonna did sometimes when she claimed that Saint Graziella came to visit her in her dreams. Saint Graziella usually told Nonna to do something that Nonna wanted to do, but no one else wanted Nonna to do. It was always

---

[1] The Botticelli Journey

a very convenient dream for Nonna.

"And so I called my brother Moe." Massimo's face waited patiently to hear the rest of this. "I think I already told you that my family run the garbage business in Greenwich?" Massimo nodded. He couldn't wait to hear the rest of her thought process. "But Moe's buddy, Pissy Pontini, has some of the routes in Port Chester!" Her voice squeaked upwards. "Don't you see?"

"I see you're nuts, Julie." He laughed and she was amazed once more at how handsome he was, his teeth white and even, his black eyes twinkling. "Pissy? What kind of a name is that?" Massimo was intrigued. "In English, doesn't that mean . . . ?"

Julie laughed too. "Everyone asks about his name. It's really Jimmy -- James, but ever since he was a little boy, he's been called 'Pissy' because he'd laugh so hard when he heard a joke that he'd wet his pants! Honest! Everyone calls him that, even his wife!" Massimo shook his head. The Americans--they were so crazy!

"So I called Moe." She continued. "He and Pissy are going to go over to 23 Evergreen Drive and they'll find out all about Annabeth and Elgin and they'll ask around and find out why they went to Italy. Just give them a few days."

"Maybe you shouldn't involve yourself in all of this," Massimo was a little uneasy. Julie talked as if this was a party, and she was in charge of the children's games. "Alessandro doesn't want you to pursue this any further." But part of him was intrigued. Why *were* those people in Malafortuna?

Julie's bottom lip was out far enough to walk on. "Alessandro doesn't own me," Massimo's eyebrows said oh yeah? to her. "No. No one tells me what to do. Come on, Massimo, we can't just let Annabeth and Elgin get butchered and not do anything about it!" She glared at him.

He recognized in her the same insatiable curiosity that came over him whenever there was a crime to figure out. She'd never give up either. He might as well join in. "You and me, Julie. We're a lot alike. We like to know what makes people tick. Alessandro, he's different. He could care less about what makes people do what they do, he only wants to make sure that he makes money hand over fist from what they do. Ha! It's too bad that you and I aren't in love with one another. We'd make a great team."

Startled, she looked at him as if for the first time. She saw something in his eyes, just behind the merry twinkle. Some glimpse of yearning, kept well tamped down. "Massimo!" She said softly. "You're in love? " He began to laugh and shook his head, no. No. "You . . . You do love someone." Her mouth dropped open and her brain churned furiously. "It's someone that . . . what?" Some glimmer opened and then, it was gone. "It's true! Who is it?" Massimo's cheeks stained red and he made some loud noises, pooh-poohing her train of thought. She watched him for a moment and then told him sincerely, "I'm sorry. I won't say anything to anyone, but I hope everything turns out well for you and that you're happy sometime."

"You are absolutely nuts. Me, I love them all. That's me. Massimo the *mammoni*. I have a girl in every town and three in between. His laugher sounded genuine, but Julie wasn't convinced. "And anyway, " he turned the subject back to the murders, "It's not like I wasn't going to do anything about the murders. I'd be glad of any information that your brother uncovered." His big hand made the motion of talking on the telephone. "I just think you shouldn't put yourself in any danger, that's all."

"You *need* my help! I can't believe that lady and I shopped at the same store and that I found her on top of that mountain for nothing! There must be *some* reason!" She forgot about Massimo's love life. Her eyes grew darker and she appealed to him. "Maybe God wants me to help."

"Mmmmm. God, huh? " He dubiously. "And Saint Graziella will appear to you tonight and explain it all to you."

Saint Graziella? She made a scrunched up face at him. What was he talking about? She shrugged again. She *had* to make him pay attention to her. "And you can solve the murder yourself. I don't want any of the glory." Relentlessly, she dangled the final carrot at him. "So you'll come out looking like a rose instead of that dorkey Chief Nargi! Maybe you'll even get a big promotion when this is all over!"

Massimo petted her on the head as if she were a kitten. "And maybe I don't *want* a big promotion, Julie. I like being a policeman right here in Malafortuna. What you'd call in America a small cheese. Although," he brooded, "I don't like the idea of someone killing two people under my nose." He slumped back into his chair and looked at her for a long moment. "All right. You can get some information from your brother and tell me. But that's *all*. Understand? *Capisci*?"

"Naturally, Massimo." And she smiled brilliantly at him and went back to the bakery to learn about making *foccacia*. And to think about who it might be that Massimo truly loved.

He watched her go. He hoped he fooled her a little. Somehow, he didn't think she was going to stop at simply supplying him with information about these people and what kind of garbage they threw away. He shrugged elaborately and his eyes began to dance. "What are you looking so happy about?" Nonna Graziella greeted him at the lunch table. "And where did you eat last night?"

"At Marina's," He kissed his grandmother's cheek. "But you knew that already, didn't you?"

Nonna Graziella made a sour face. "I heard she made *giambotta*. Was it as good as mine?"

"It was all right."

"Hmpf. She's a good cook. Not as good as me, but a good cook." She glared at Massimo suspiciously. "But don't forget, she's off limits to a Romeo like you." Massimo rolled his eyes. "She's still a married woman. Don't get any ideas!"

"You have a disgusting mind, Nonna. Don't worry about me." He sat down eagerly for lunch. Nonna had prepared him *linguini* with fresh tuna fish sauce.

✦ ✦ ✦

Kneading a huge mass of dough was a good physical task for leaving one's mind open for thinking. Julie punched the sticky mass, picking it up and slapping it down hard on the breadboard with her right hand. Her left hand was left free to sprinkle the flour, a little at a time, onto the dough and breadboard. *What* should she do? *What* should she do? The rhythm drummed in her brain. On the one hand, she was crazy about him. His touch enflamed her, and, if he kissed her for more than one or two minutes, she'd be mush and be unable to stop. She scooped up the entire dough mass and slammed it down. On the other hand, he was definitely not the kind of man she wanted to want. Much too opinionated, trying to tell her what to do. And he cared too much for outward appearances. He was selfish and insensitive. She slammed the dough back down again. *But he's really been trying to be nicer, hasn't he? He's been hanging around Malafortuna, hasn't he? He's been really nice to his mother and grandmother, hasn't he? He even took his grandmother to the doctor's office today, didn't he?* She dribbled a little flour over the dough. *Yeah, but he's only doing that because he wants you to think he's a better person. That way, he'll talk you into letting him into your pants.*

The man's the president of a huge corporation, for God's sake, she told herself. *He can run rings around you. Yeah, but you'd like to have him in your pants, wouldn't you?* Her face flamed. It certainly was hot in here and she was kneading vigorously. That was why her cheeks were so pink, wasn't it?

Zara came over to see how she was doing. She poked a finger into the dough and nodded encouragingly. "It's hard work getting through it, but it's so rewarding when you finish." She clapped Julie on the shoulder and went to pull some loaves from the oven.

Julie thought about what Zara had said. The dough was massing together nicely, becoming shiny and supple under her hands. She continued to knead and think. *If I give in to him, I'll just be one more conquest. She could hear him laughing to his friends, "She was an American," he'd brag, "Yeah, they're easy."* She frowned at the dough and stuck two fingers in it fiercely, as if she were stabbing Alessandro in the eyes. Never! She'd never be easy! She picked up then entire slab of dough and slammed it down. No, dammit. She'd never give in until he asked her to marry him! Never!

She stopped punching the dough and looked at it in wonder. What had she been thinking? Did she want to *marry* Alessandro? Zara came over again, dusting of her floury hands. "Beautiful," she admired the silken texture. "I think you're ready to begin shaping it now."

He spoke several times to his office. They were getting along fine without his presence there. Salvatore Giotopolous had done a fine job, getting the contract signed and the terms that they had wanted. It was about time that he gave more responsibility to his eager assistant. "Give yourself a raise, Salvatore . . . . Yes, yes, I mean it. The account is yours now, all yours . . . and . . . who? . . . No, you handle it. Of course I mean everything I'm saying. Not only that, but you'll have to handle the Maserati thing too. I won't be able to leave here until next week . . . It's very hush-hush, you understand . . . Yes, the head of the Police . . . Yes. I realize, but what can I do in the face of such officialdom? Thanks, Salvatore. I knew I could rely on you."

Kendra was harder. He could hear her pouts over the telephone. "I'll be back as soon as I can. Tuesday, the latest . . .I'm glad you went. Who did you take? Ah, did she enjoy it? Good . . . . Good . . . . Me, too . . . . Of course I do." He turned to see his mother standing in the kitchen, listening to him with suspicion. She'd heard the whole damn conversation! *Merde!* He glared at his mother, trying to ward off his own guilt and stalked off to find Julie.

He'd been royally annoyed last night when she kissed him and closed the door in his face. Who the hell did she think she was? He sputtered a good morning to Signora Biasi, barely acknowledging her as he walked to Marina's house. No one ever turned down his advances. Why look how Kendra wanted him back in Milano! He snorted to himself. Get real, Alessi, he muttered to himself, Kendra is a self-serving bimba. Julie is . . . sweet . . . and soft . . . and feisty . . . and beautiful. He'd spent most of the night thinking about her. By his side, riding in the car. Next to him at dinner. In bed, with her copper hair in wild disarray. Waking her with a soft kiss in the early morning sunshine and then waking her in other ways. He wanted her. But not just her body. No, he wanted everything. Julie in the morning, Julie at night. She'd always be a good mother to their children . . . . He stopped and stood still for a minute. Was he losing his mind? Children? Hadn't he been hurt enough? Enough of thinking of Julie! He schooled his brain to think about the upcoming Maserati negotiations. But the shadowy images of two little girls with curly reddish hair tied with ribbons came popping through the rows of numbers he was calculating. Children. He took the thoughts out in the open and mulled over them until he arrived at his sister's house.

Anton was at Julie's little table, working hard at his homework. Alessandro swallowed his disappointment. Was he never going to see Julie alone, ever again? Anton spoke to him in English, "I think she's at the bakery. Do you want me to go and get her? I could take your car again." Anton's dark eyes lit up.

"No. Thanks, Anton." The new name seemed natural already. "I'll just sit and wait." He wandered out on Julie's terrace and sat down on a chair, thinking that Anton's English had certainly improved. Julie's lessons with him were working wonders. "Ahhhh." He propped his feet up on the railing and sat in the sun, doing nothing for the first time in more than fifteen years. It felt good. His eyes closed and his mind went blank.

✦ ✦ ✦

Moe hopped into Pissy's red and black garbage truck and the two of them, like demented caricatures of secret agent men, roared off to Evergreen Drive. They'd been good buddies all through their lives, best friends in high school and the two of them had worked every summer as helpers on Moe's father's truck. Moe had stood up for Pissy and his wife Mary when they got married and Geraldine, Pissy's oldest daughter, was Moe's godchild.

When Moe took over running the company when his father retired, Pissy was his manager. And when one of the routes in Port Chester opened up, Moe's father had loaned Pissy the money to buy it, along with Pissy's first truck. The loan had been long since paid, but the gratitude for the friendship and generosity would remain forever in Pissy's sturdy, loyal heart.

Number 23 turned out to be a conservative older home in a neat, prosperous, well-settled neighborhood. "It's not my route, it belongs to Eddie Cacchiatore. Remember him?" Moe nodded. "He's had these people as customers for more than 20 years, most of them. He knew the Stanleys. They'd been here for a couple of years." Pissy jumped up and down on his high perch. "This is our chance, pal. We'll be just like real live detectives."

Moe leaned over and tooted the horn. "That's us! Here come the G-men! Watch out, criminals, 'cause here comes Moe and Pissy!" The two of them laughed like schoolboys.

And indeed, not really being a G-man was probably Moe's only disappointment in life. He'd always ached to be a policeman, dreaming dreams of catching the bad guys and wearing the blue uniform and the silver badge. But, as his father's only son, his destiny was to take over the business and become a garbage man. He always referred to himself as a 'G-man', pretending that he was really a detective in disguise. "An' after all, Pis," he said many times, "No cop can have more knowledge of what makes our customers tick. Who knows more about the people they serve than us G-men?"

Pissy also shared the boyhood dreams. "Right you are. We know what they read, what they drink, what their bank statements look like . . . Everything!"

"Yeah, and coming so early in the morning, we know who stays over and who doesn't, we know what medicines they take, and whether they're clean and neat or pigs." Moe laughed. "Show me a man's garbage pails and I can tell you all about his soul!"

They parked the truck at the curb in front of the house. Pissy and Moe got out of the truck and walked up the paving stones that led to the house next door. "Eddie said their names are Fitzsimmons. He said to use his name." He rang the doorbell. Pissy took off his Yankees hat. "Mrs. Fitzsimmons? Hi. I'm James Pontini. I'm a refuse collector here in Port Chester. Eddie Cacchiatore, your refuse collector, said you might be able to help us in a matter of great importance."

"Eddie! You're friends with Eddie? Come on in." Mrs. Fitzsimmons was a jolly freckled lady with frizzy pepper and salt hair. She brought them into the living room, talking over her shoulder. "Eddie is terrific. He helped me out a few years ago when I had a dead squirrel in my toilet." The men looked at her in surprise and she kept on talking as she pointed to the couch and let herself down into a big leather covered chair. "I didn't know what to do or who to call and there he was, emptying the garbage pails and so I said, 'Eddie, help me. There's a squirrel in my toilet.' And he came right up and took care of it."

"How'd you get a dead squirrel in your toilet?" Moe asked politely.

She laughed merrily, making her chins wobble. "I simply don't know! Isn't it amazing? I was so upset," she put her hand over her heart, "But Eddie just fished it out. He's an angel. And did he ever tell you about making my son, Harry, give up his pacifier? " Pissy nodded. "Well, then you know why Eddie's family with us. If you're a friend of Eddie's, then you're a friend of mine! Now, how can I help you?"

Moe sat forward in the squishy sofa and told her what his sister had said. Mrs. Fitzsimmons listened and tears rolled out of her eyes. "She was such a nice neighbor. It was such a shock, you know, when the police came here and told us." She sniffed. "They never asked us any questions about her, just said that the two of them had died in an accident." She sniffed again. "And they were so stiff and formal, I wouldn't have told them any gossip, but you two are friends of Eddie's." She popped up and asked them if they wanted coffee and then, whisked off to the kitchen before they could even answer.

"What's the story about the pacifiers?" Moe whispered. Pissy chuckled and began to relate the story. Just then, Mrs. Fitzsimmons came in with three mugs of coffee on a tray.

"You boys drink up and I'll tell you all about the letter the Stanleys got and why they went to that horrible foreign place." She perched on the arm of the sofa, looking like a frisky squirrel herself. "Well, about three months ago, Annabeth got a funny letter from this priest. He told her that she had inherited a farm in Italy from her mother's brother, I think. The priest sent the uncle's Will in the letter and the name of her relative . . . I can't recall the name . . . " She looked up at the ceiling of her room for inspiration, but then shook her frizzled head. "I can't remember, but I think it started with an "O". Oscar?" she mused. "No. Maybe it wasn't an "O". I'm sorry," she spread her hands out in distress. Moe told her that she was being very helpful and not to worry if she couldn't remember.

"Just relax and maybe it will come back to you." He soothed.

She shrugged. "Ah well, so Annabeth and Elgin wrote back and said that they were coming to Italy." She picked up her coffee cup and took a sip, trying to think back. "I got the impression that they planned to stay with this cousin." A sudden tear trickled down her cheek. "Annabeth was even joking that they might like Italy so much that they'd stay there! Oh, this is such a terrible and sad thing!"

❖ ❖ ❖

Anton sat Julie's table, a pencil stuck in his mouth, trying to decline past participles. It was late afternoon. Julie had been gone most of the day, spending it with Zia Nina, learning how to wrap the soft goat cheese with leaves and herbs and then how to store them to ripen, stacked carefully in woven baskets while the whey dripped out and made them firm. In the middle of the lessons, Zia Nina had mentioned several times that Alessandro had taken his mother to Torriano to have a corn removed from her left big toe. "He's behaving like a proper son should," Zia said firmly watching Julie's face to see what her reaction might be. Each time, Julie nodded dutifully and later Zia would tell Zio Nunzio that the romance seemed to be proceeding well. Zio Nunzio remarked that Julie was too good a catch for Alessandro. "We should write to our cousins in America and see if they want to meet up with her when she goes back."

"She's not going anywhere," Zia Nina made a face at him. "She's proceeding very well with Alessandro Alessi."

❖ ❖ ❖

Julie wasn't quite as sure that it was progressing that well. She hadn't seen Alessandro since the night before last. Yesterday afternoon, she hadn't known that Alessandro had come to her house, and when Zara and Teodora asked her to stay for supper, she'd agreed. Alessandro had waked from his nap, waited for another hour for Julie to come home, and then, in sheer frustration, eaten dinner alone at La Famiglia. He had, obviously, taken his mother with him this morning, and Julie hadn't a clue as to when he'd be back. She left Anton muttering and twisting the lock of hair that fell over his eye. Past participle declensions held no interest for her and she went downstairs to use Marina's phone. She called Massimo. "Come on over. I have news for you." She waited for him upstairs on her terrace.

He strolled over and, from her perch on the terrace, she watched him come down the street. First, for some reason, he stopped downstairs at Marina's apartment. The door was never locked and he poked his head inside. The kitchen sat, shiny and clean and empty, smelling of herbs and flowers. He sucked at his lower lip, looking like a pup that had lost his bone. He'd been hoping that Marina would have been home and that maybe she would have asked him to stay again for dinner. Mamma was making lentil soup, never one of Massimo's favorites. He sniffed hopefully at the big pot on the stove. Sauce with spareribs. He stuck one finger into the sauce and tasted it. *Meraviglioso.* Massimo plodded upstairs. He'd hang around until suppertime. Maybe Marina would take pity on him then and ask him to stay.

Julie sat at the little straw table, meticulously applying pale pink polish to her toenails. *"Ciao,* Massimo."

" *'Giorno,* Julie. What's the news from America?"

Julie told him. "And so she told Moe and Pissy everything. They'd been neighbors for several years. Annabeth was so excited about coming to Italy. She had gotten this letter from some old man telling her that she was his heir. The old man's sister --or was it his aunt-- oh, some relation, had come to America years and years ago when the family had some kind of a feud. Mrs. Fitzsimmons wasn't too clear about it all, but anyway, she did say that Annabeth never even knew that she still had any relatives in Italy. Then, when the letter came, she was delighted and surprised." Julie leaned backwards, waving her foot in the air to dry the polish on her toes. Massimo took out a piece of paper and began scribbling notes as Julie talked.

"On the letter, on the margin, there was a hand-written note mentioning the name Oscar, or Omar or some name that began with an 'O'. Annabeth showed everything to Mrs. Fitzsimmons; that's how she was sure of all of this part. The note was in Italian of course, but the old man's letter told them what it said." Julie was so excited that she sat up with the nail polish brush in her hand, waving it for emphasis. "Maybe it said 'Otto'! Like Otto the horrible, that man that lives near the church and is so awful to everyone! Did his uncle leave him a farm?"

Massimo nodded, getting excited in spite of himself.

Julie nearly danced around the terrace. "That's it! He killed them! The note said that Otto or Omar or Oscar or whatever would sure be surprised that the farm and the house had been left to the sister and thereafter to her children or child --that was Annabeth, as you well know." Massimo nodded, trying hard to follow Julie's enthusiastic explanation. "So Annabeth and her husband--listen to this, Massimo --*wrote to this guy telling him that they were coming out to see him and see the farm and that they might--if they liked it-- settle down on the farm when they retired!*" Her grey eyes sparked and danced. "So *Otto* must have *killed* them!"

Massimo's heart beat a little faster. Could it be? Otto? He considered it. Otto certainly was a miserable bastard. Everyone knew that. But could he murder anyone? Massimo's head nodded up and down without even thinking. Certainly, if money was involved. Otto would be stuck like a pig in a sausage factory if all this were true. He tried to look at Julie's information from all sides. "Did the Stanleys leave a copy of the letter at home?"

"No. Or if they did, Mrs. Fitzsimmons couldn't find it. She had a key to the Stanley's house and she looked through everything with Moe and Pissy. They couldn't find anything at all that referred to anything. No notes, nothing. Mrs. Fitzsimmons thought that they maybe took all the papers with them when they came here. Don't you see? He killed them for sure."

"Maybe," Massimo said slowly. "But we have no proof. We don't even know that it's the right name! It could be anyone who had a name beginning with "O". Oratzio Lanterna . . . or Ottavio Tripodi . . . ." He shrugged his shoulders awkwqardly. "There's Obrigiano LaVersa, out on the farm on the mountain . . . and, um, Orso Mariana, except I think he moved to the south . . . I can think of more, too. I mean, Otto isn't the only one." Julie made an exasperated sound. "And how would we know that Otto or any of them received any letter from the Stanleys?" He scratched his head. "Chief Nargi has been in contact with the police from the United States. They looked around in the house, too, according to him. There was some correspondence with a travel agency for the tickets and car rental, but nothing more. Nothing about a letter, nothing about a Will. Nothing about an Oscar or an Otto or a Ozatzio." He made a nonchalant face, but secretly, he was excited inside.

Julie made a face too. "So what? The neighbors didn't tell any of this to the American police. So how would they know anything to tell Nargi? Annabeth *must* have written to Otto. It *had* to be him! He's such a miserable excuse for a human being." Her eyes shone as she visualized the drama "He would have been bleeding in his spaghetti sauce when he got her letter. He would have been in a panic. He'd already sold the house and the farm to those Tuscan Estate people. He'd be in a horrible position if Annabeth had really been the heir and not him!"

"Maybe. Calm down. What else did Moe say?"

"Well, he and Pissy talked it over and tried to make up a plausible scenario of what might have happened. Let's say that the Stanleys told Otto they were coming out here. That's certainly possible, isn't it?" Massimo made a face and Julie rushed on. "Then Otto would make plans to meet them somewhere. Maybe he'd tell them to bring all the papers with them. And then he *butchered* them!" She beseeched him, "Otherwise, why would they ever be coming out here? It must have been like that. You have to admit it all sounds plausible!" She bared her teeth, looking like an avenging alley cat. "That lady *shopped* with me! I want him caught!"

Reluctantly, Massimo nodded. "It could be. It could be any of those "O" people, or maybe even another letter of the alphabet." He grinned suddenly, "But it was someone, wasn't it? And Nargi doesn't know anything at all about this part."

"And we won't tell him. He's such an arrogant little poop. So nasty to you when you could solve the whole thing. So nasty to me, trying to pin the blame on me and putting you down in front of everyone." She stood up suddenly and began to prowl around the terrace. "We need to find the proof. We need the letters."

"If there are any letters," Massimo was cautious. "And everything else – their other clothes --where are they?" He, too, in his mind envisioned Otto as a criminal. "Would he destroy everything? And how about her ring? She had some kind of a ring on. I could see where Otto ripped it off her finger! And a necklace. The killer tore it off her neck. He'd only take the ring and the necklace if he planned to keep them, right? Maybe there are more things from Fancy's. And their luggage and stuff."

Julie made a wailing noise. "How can we get into his house and search?"

"Let's not leap so far ahead, Julie. Everyone hates Otto, but it might be some other name. Maybe it wasn't even a name beginning with an 'O'. Let's not get excited." Julie gave him a scornful look. Massimo tried to placate her. "If I give this information to Nargi-- and I should give it to him as a representative of the law --we'll get a *mandato di perquistzione* and then we'll be able to search his house legally."

"And give Nargi all the credit? No! Let's try to do it ourselves!" Julie gave him her best pleading look, "Come on. Let's at least try."

"Otto would never allow anyone to question him or search for any evidence without a *mandato*. It's a public document and Otto would find out about it when the request was made. If any sniff of this got to him, he'd destroy everything before we could catch him." Massimo looked gloomy. "And it might not be Otto. It could be almost anyone. We'll have to leave it to Nargi."

She stood at the table, dejection written all over her face. Massimo stared back at her sadly. The image of himself, making an arrest single-handedly, without Nargi's pompous presence, filled his head. He'd be a hero. Maybe decorated with a medal for his courage and intelligence. The picture became brighter. He was on a balcony. There were admiring crowds below, cheering and whistling. The *Governatore* shook his hand and pinned the medal on his chest. And Nargi had to stand in the background grinding his teeth and pretending to be pleased. He could feel Marina looking up at him with pride and . . . and what? The dream burst back into reality. He shook his head again slowly, "No. We just can't get into Otto's house or anyone else's house without making them suspicious."

"But I can." They whirled, startled. They'd forgotten Anton, sitting so quietly just inside the door, doing his homework. "I could get into the house and look for the clothing and documents."

"You?" Massimo sputtered. "Otto hates kids. He'd never let you in."

"He would if I was being punished for damaging his terraces like I did Julie's," He grinned at them. "I'll just become a bad boy again. I'll overturn his flowerpots and break a few things." Julie's mouth dropped open and her eyes goggled. "He'll make a big complaint and he'll call you in, Massimo. You'll catch me and I'll be very sorry, just like I was with Julie." His face was alight with glee. "You'll be very stern with me, Massimo. You'll make me work for him after school for ten days. I'd have to do whatever he wanted me to do . . . scrub his floors and do . . . whatever he wants me to do for punishment. That way I'll be in the house and he won't suspect anything. He's such a miser that he'll be happy to have someone slave away for free, and who would suspect a thirteen year old boy?" He straightened up to his full height. "Well, a nearly fourteen year old boy, of trying to search the house?"

Julie and Massimo looked at each other. "Brilliant!" She said, and the three of them began to laugh hysterically.

"No, Anton," Julie said soberly, after they had stopped laughing. "This is a vicious killer. We can't let you be in any danger for this, even to catch him. It might not be Otto. It could be someone from another village. I could be 'way off base." Both Massimo and Anton looked at her, trying to figure out the meaning of the American baseball phrase. Julie went on, relentlessly. "Your mother would kill me double dead if anything happened to you." She shook her head dejectedly. "Thanks, honey-bunch. It was a good idea. But whoever he is, he's already murdered two people over this matter already and if it is Otto, he's so mean that he wouldn't balk at killing one more. No. *Absolutely no.* We'll just have to think and find another way."

"But, Julie . . . " He remonstrated. "I can do it safely. There won't be any danger." Julie shook her head violently.

"Ab-so-lute-ly *No!*" She appealed to Massimo. "We can't put him into any danger, right?" Massimo nodded reluctantly. It wasn't so much the medal that he wanted, it was the thought of Marina's adulation. But if anything happened to Anton! No. No. He shook his head reluctantly at the boy. Anton's disappointment was nearly palpable. His bottom lip stuck out slightly and had Julie been less excited, she might have noticed that he looked as muleish as she did when she wanted her own way and planned to get it, no matter what.

"Right," Massimo sighed. He got up from the chair. "Let me think about it all. Maybe something else will come up. Maybe they'll find something if they search the house in Port Arthur again." He said good-bye sadly to Julie, too depressed to even think of staying any longer. Then, turning his body so that Julie couldn't see his face, he said good-bye to Anton, letting him see the wink and conspiratorial expression on his face. "Let's all keep our wits about us and something might just come up."

CHAPTER TEN

"You just missed Alessandro's call," Marina told Julie. "Mamma's foot doctor wants to finish removing her corn tomorrow morning. He put some salve on it today to soften the corn and she's going to stay tonight with Alessandro at his apartment. They'll be back in the afternoon."

"Tomorrow! And *I'm* going to Torriano tomorrow afternoon to work with Luisa at her restaurant," Julie pushed the stab of disappointment down. She didn't want Marina to know how much she wanted to see her brother. She felt depressed over the whole situation.

Marina prepared a wonderful meal that evening, eggplant rolled around a savory *ricotta* stuffing slathered with Marina's leftover sparerib sauce. The food tasted like sawdust to Julie. She excused herself and went to bed early. It was a mistake, as the night seemed endless and sleep eluded her for hours. She wondered what Alessandro was doing in Milano. Was he missing her as much as she missed him?

✦ ✦ ✦

He took Mamma to a Chinese restaurant. She enjoyed the fun of the different food, even trying to use chopsticks. It had been a splendid day. She'd enjoyed his company all day long. For the first time since he had moved away, he hadn't been trying to convince her to move to the city with him. As a matter of fact, he expressed an unusual interest in what he referred to as 'the old days', asking her eager questions about her father, her grandparents, and what life had been like when she'd grown up in Malafortuna. He wanted to know everything. All the little details that he'd never been interested enough to ask about before.

She settled herself comfortably in his big leather chair, ready to talk and talk. Maybe Alessandro might share a little of himself with her tonight. Perhaps even tell her about what he was feeling for Julie. It was wonderful to see Alessandro so . . . well, like the boy that he once was, without all the stiff veneer that he had put on since he left home. The telephone rang, it's shrill voice interrupting her story of how Nonno Alessi had met Nonna on the night that the gypsies came to Malafortuna. And then her evening was marred.

He tried to keep her from hearing any of it, but she knew it was that woman that Signora DiZito, the doctor's wife, had seen him with one night. She knew she was pretty, and a bleached blonde. Signora DiZito didn't know any more than that.

"Mamma, I'm going out for an hour or so. Make yourself at home. Watch television, if you want. Don't wait up for me. I'll see you in the morning." He kissed the top of her head, but didn't meet her eyes.

❖ ❖ ❖

"So what's the story with Eddie and the pacifier?" Moe and Pissy were splitting a white clam pizza.

"That Eddie, what a legend!" Pissy scooped up a tasty piece of clam between his fingers and popped it into his mouth. "He was on the route one morning, early, and this lady came out of the house with her two year old kid. It was one of those ritzy houses, up in the Polo Club area," Moe nodded, picking up another slice. "The lady was yelling, "Eddie! Eddie! Stop!". So Eddie stopped the truck. The lady came running up and she winked a big wink at Eddie. 'Eddie', she says, 'Show little Billy here how he can throw away his pacifier!'. Eddie hasn't got the faintest idea of what she's talkin' about. She keeps winking at him and making a face, like this," and Pissy made a hideous moue. "She says, 'You remember, Eddie, how the little boy down the street threw his pacifier into the back of your garbage truck? Huh, Eddie, you remember, don't ya?' So Eddie all of a sudden catches on to what the lady is trying to do." Moe looked blank. "She was trying to get her kid to throw away his pacifier! See? And she wanted Eddie to help her."

Moe nodded reluctantly, "I guess so."

Pissy finished his piece of pizza. "You want the last slice?" He asked Moe hopefully. Moe shook his head. No. Pissy slid the slice onto his plate and added a shake of red pepper. "So Eddie catches on. He says, 'Oh, yeah,

Mrs. Whatsyourname. I remember now.'. And Mrs. Whatsyourname looks like the sun came out in her face. She told Eddie to open the door and come on out. She wanted him to be at the back of the truck when little Bobby throws his pacifier into the garbage."

"I thought you said the kid's name was Billy?"

"Billy, Bobby, who cares, Moe. That's not the point of the story." Pissy was patient. "So, then, Eddie gets out of the truck and walks back to the business end. The kid has this pacifier pluggin' up his mouth. The lady uses this high voice, 'Throw the pacifier into the truck, Billy, or Bobby, or whatever the hell the kid's name was.' " Pissy's voice was a shrill falsetto and several customers of the Pizzeria looked around to see who was talking like that. "And the kid throws the pacifier into the business end. Eddie shows the kid how to push the button to make the arm sweep the garbage inta the truck, and bye-bye to the pacifier. The kid and the lady and Eddie all wave good bye to it."

"Good story, Pissy. Eddie is a brilliant guy!"

"That's not the end, Moe." Pissy looked slightly annoyed. "There's more." Moe sat back down and tried to pick up a few crumbs from the pizza tin with his finger. "Then the lady wanted Eddie to let the kid ride up front with him to the end of the driveway. You now, sort of as a reward for being such a big boy."

"Is that the end?"

"Nah. Not even close. Remember, Eddie is a *legend!* The lady told everybody. And *all* the lady mothers on the street, and then all the lady mothers in the town --It was incredible, Moe. They all made Eddie show their kid how to throw away their pacifiers. He was a legend, Moe. A legend."

"Good story, Pis. Can we go now?" Moe was laughing.

"Sure, Moe. I just wanted you to understand why that lady told us whatever we wanted to know. Because of Eddie." He shook his head in admiration.

"A legend." Moe tossed a twenty on the table. It was plenty for the bill and a good tip for the waitress. His face was wreathed in admiration for Eddie. "I understand now," Moe assured Pissy. "He's a legend."

✦ ✦ ✦

If she'd known how badly Alessandro's evening was going to go, Sofia might have slept a little better. For the first time in many years, Alessandro was having a wonderful time talking with her. He'd never heard some of her stories, and all of a sudden, it seemed like the most important thing in the world to find out how Nonna and Nonno met. He was surprisingly starved for a quiet night, with only his mother to talk with. And then, when the two of them had shared a bottle of wine, he would have been happy to have gone peacefully to sleep, with Julie's smile in his heart.

"Maybe tomorrow. " He tried to wiggle out of her invitation gracefully, but Kendra was insistent that he come over. Right that minute. She'd dashed to her closet, kicked off the bathrobe she was wearing, and put on the special thing that she had bought today. Bright red. The most expensive negligee in the shop. It was a sensation and the salesclerk had guaranteed that it would make anyone sit up and beg. She fluffed the marabou feathers dyed to match stitched to the neckline. Her tiny feet wiggled into high-heeled slippers exactly the same red as the negligee, with absurd pom-poms made of feathers on the toes. She preened at herself in the long mirror. The salesclerk was right. He'd never be able to resist her tonight.

She made a quick telephone call, hoping to line up the man downstairs for tomorrow night, but there was no one at home. She left a very graphic message. She'd certainly had a wonderful time with him. He hadn't been Alessandro. Nor did he have one-tenth of Alessandro's money. But he had been a very willing participant in a few nighttime activities that she particularly enjoyed. Right from the start, she'd been perceptive enough to sense Alessandro would have drawn back, disgusted, if she had ever suggested any of them to him. She shrugged her pretty shoulders. She'd find time for them both, and Alessandro would never find out. He hadn't found out about the waiter at the Indian Restaurant, had he? Or Leonardo, the actor? Or the boy who delivered her groceries. She laughed; men were so stupid! She'd be sure to make him feel terrible for leaving her on her own that night. Maybe pressure him to buy her a gold bracelet or a ring to make up for his inattentiveness.

"I missed you the other night. My girlfriend wasn't very good company." She managed to look woebegone, desirable and dejected all at the same time. Alessandro apologized handsomely, wanting only to go home.

"You were so mean not to come back," she pouted. "All I did was cry because you went away, my darling." He apologized again. "How are you going to make it up to me?" She wound her arms around him and deliberately ground her pelvis against him. Usually, this would arouse him, but he only looked at her with detached eyes. She really was a *bimba*, he thought. She looked like a slut. The nightgown was straight out of a bad movie, and the shoes could have been worn by someone in a bordello. Kendra's practiced sex fared badly with his memory of Julie, in the field of hay, clutching the little white goat to her neck.

She sensed his distaste and was puzzled. Why wasn't he responding? "Come on, darling." Her voice purred at him. "Be nice to me. You left me here, all by myself and I was so lonely for your touch." She pulled him closer and kissed him. Her breasts pressed against him and the smell of her heavy perfume wrapped around his senses. He wanted no part of her, but she touched him expertly and he began to respond. "That's better," she whispered and then she dropped to her knees. His body reacted to her touches and he reached down for her, just as she knew he would. The phone rang. "Let it ring, darling."

The bell shrilled four times more and then the answering machine clicked on. Her rhythmical movements stilled suddenly as the caller's voice left his message. Alessandro listened to the man's voice for a moment and then pushed Kendra away.

She began to babble. "It's a mistake. I don't even know who it is. Alessandro, listen to me. *Listen! Alessandro!*" But he was already out the door.

✦ ✦ ✦

"She's at Luisa's for the day," Anton explained. "She'll be back in the morning."

He shrugged good-naturedly . He missed her like crazy and it had only been a day. "Come on," he beckoned to his nephew. "Let's you and me have a driving lesson." And Anton's grin of delight almost made up for Julie's absence.

They took the Ferrari high up in the hills and Anton drove with sheer pleasure, letting the powerful car zoom through the valleys, nearly missing chickens and goats on the side of the road. Alessandro showed him how to double-clutch on the sharp turns, how to let the mechanical perfection of the engine and gears, made by Alessi of course, take the car effortlessly wherever one wanted it to go. "Zio, I'd give anything for a car like this," Anton sighed.

"All you need is a lot of money, Anton." Alessandro smiled fondly at the boy whom he barely knew a week ago, "You'll work hard and get one someday." He sat back, letting Anton experiment with the car's abilities.

"This car," he patted the soft leather of the dashboard, "It represents my success." He spotted a *trattoria* at the bottom of the road. "Let's stop for some food, Anton." Anton drove expertly into the restaurant and stopped with a spurt of gravel in front of the arched entryway. Three old men sitting at a table under the trees watched them as they took chairs at a nearby table. The waiter came up and took their orders. The three old men got up and circled the Ferrari, silently looking at the controls and watching their reflections in the shiny red fenders. Anton began to giggle.

"In a million years, Anton, they'd never earn enough to buy half the car," Alessandro told him. "But maybe they are happier men than I am." Anton's eyes snapped to his uncle's face. "I'm slowly learning." Alessandro savored his glass of wine, "That too much money isn't the answer to life. I've been living in a false world, where values are turned upside down. These men, perhaps they live in a better world."

"But maybe they're mean and selfish and beat their wives, Zio. Just because a man is poor doesn't make him noble either," Anton picked up a piece of *calamari* and popped it into his mouth. "Me, I'd like to be rich and a good person, too." His uncle laughed, marveling at the innocent intelligent wisdom in front of him.

They ate and talked and Alessandro told his nephew about what it was like to be the smartest boy ever to go to Malafortuna School. And how it was to travel from Malafortuna to Milano. "I knew I was going a long way, but I didn't realize how the journey affected me. I made a lot of mistakes, Anton, trying to become successful and adult. I made a bad marriage. Some of it was her fault, some of it mine. I just wasn't mature enough to understand. Confusing success with maturity." Anton looked puzzled, but Alessandro kept on talking. "And I kept on making mistakes. Like being ashamed of Mamma and Nonna and the way they lived. I turned my back on you and your mother and my friend Renzo. And why? Because you all stayed back here and didn't want the things I thought were so important."

"I think a lot of those things are important, Zio." Anton stubbornly clung to his own opinions, "You see Malafortuna through the eyes of your wealth. You find it charming and unspoiled." He shook his head. "But there are bad things here too in the simplicity. Things that make it hard for Mamma to hold her head up because she was deserted by my father." Anton's face was a dull red and Alessandro felt a pain in his stomach for the boy's hurt. "And Chiara, my friend. The good and simple people spit down at her because they don't know if she has a father or how she was conceived. And her mother and Zara. Chiara loves them both, but no one in Malafortuna understands, and, Chiara herself doesn't understand." He gave a little laugh, "And to tell the honest truth, Zio, *I* don't understand either. I . . . I can't quite figure out why two women . . . and then . . . Chiara starts to cry." His face was a study in despair. "And then I think, 'What kind of a person are you, Anton. They are good and kind and loving people, Zara and Teodora.' But their relationship is . . . confusing, Zio. And makes even their daughter sometimes sad." He sighed.

"It's a funny world, Anton. I have no answers for you." Alessandro touched Anton's hand. "But if Zara and Chiara's mother love one another and their love is selfless and good, well, then they are lucky. Even if people don't understand." He mused quietly. "We all want to find true love." He scratched his ear, "And even if you can find it, sometimes you don't know just what to do with it." The waiter appeared, holding two plates of *spaghetti*, drenched in oily, red sauce. "Ahhhh, let's eat." And their philosophical wonderings were pushed back by the delicious food in front of them.

While they ate, Alessandro told Anton stories about Malafortuna in his own youth. "You think you are bad," he laughed, "But Renzo and I --we were even worse." He considered his nephew. "Do you remember hearing about the goat that was left in church?"

"The goat?" Anton goggled at him. "That was *you?*"

"Father Lovallo was always yelling at us. We were probably the worst altar boys Malafortuna had ever known, spilling the wine, *drinking* the wine, snorting and laughing during Mass, you name it, we did it." He chortled, thinking back. "We'd done something, God only knows what. I don't even remember. But we vowed to get even with Father Lovallo. One night, we went up to Gaetano's farm. Everyone in town hated him and we figured we'd kill two birds with a single stone. We stole his mean, old breeding goat. We had to tackle the goat and tie him up, and that's a whole other story." Anton began to giggle helplessly. "Anyway, we got the goat back to the church and pushed it in. We tied it to the altar, with a rope long enough to be sure that it could go *everywhere* in the church and make mischief, but strong enough so that it couldn't get away. The goat shit and pissed all over the church." He rubbed his hand in front of his mouth, trying to keep his laughter inside. "And it was a raunchy old thing, with urine that smelled --well, it smelled like a raunchy old goat!" Laughter started to bubble out. "Then, the next morning was Sunday and there was a big Mass. When the people came in, the whole church was covered with goat shit - the steps, the altar, the seats - everything. Father Lovallo was apoplectic. He was trying to catch the goat, and sliding on the goat shit, and everyone in the congregation was laughing." His mind's eye looked back on the scene and his expression of pure satisfaction made him look like a boy of ten again.

When they got back into the car, the three old men waved good-bye to them, solemnly saluting their good taste in automobiles.

❖ ❖ ❖

She'd dreamed about him the entire night. And here he was, sitting at his sister's table when she came down to breakfast. "Alessandro!" She couldn't hide the shaft of delight that lit up her face.

He grinned, looking exactly like his nephew. "Can I kidnap you for lunch? I have some telephone calls to make this morning, but I thought we might go on a picnic, up in the mountains, and this time, not find any dead people." His dark eyes danced. She nodded with happy laughter.

"I'm helping at the bakery this morning, but I can sneak out whenever you're ready. Can I bring anything?"

"A loaf of bread that you made with your own hands." Why did his simple words send such a jolt of heat to her midsection?

She told Teodora that she was leaving early. "I have a picnic lunch date."

"With Alessandro?" Julie nodded, trying to keep from looking like she'd swallowed a star. "I think you like him a lot, no? He's a good man," Teodora told her. "Better than some around here even know about." Julie's face was curious.

"Do you care for him, truly?" Teodora asked her. Julie nodded. Teodora busied herself folding cardboard boxes and Julie began to help her. "When I was pregnant with Chiara, I . . . ." She stopped for a moment, holding a stack of boxes in her arms. "Why I'm telling you this, I'll never know. No one else except Zara ever heard this story." She started folding the boxes mechanically, looking out into the store. "I left Malafortuna because I knew I was . . . well, you know, a lesbian." Julie started to speak but Teodora hushed her. "It was such a small village. I knew I couldn't stay and have a happy life here. I went to Milano, thinking I'd hide in the crowds. That no one in the city would care what I was like. It was hard, even there, and I tried hard to fit in. I'd always been shy, but I tried hard to make some friends. One night, I went to a party, and there was this man there. He was an arrogant bore, one of those men who can't believe you're not attracted to him. One of those guys that thinks, 'If only she had a good man, a real man, like me, she'd change. One good screw from me--she'd forget women and be normal'. He was that kind of a person." She rolled her eyes and she and Julie laughed gently. The two of them worked together in perfect harmony as the stack of boxes grew higher and higher.

"I'd had a little too much to drink and made the mistake of letting him take me home. I thought I'd be safe with him. He raped me." Julie moaned with sympathy and took Teodora's hands in her. Wryly, Teodora continued. "I discovered I was pregnant. Me! A lesbian! Pregnant by a man whose name I didn't even know. A *cretino* with sperm!"

"I didn't know what to do. I had no money and didn't know anyone who could help me. I was in despair. I thought that I'd abort the baby and I began to try to find someone who knew where I could go. I was showing, my belly was sticking out, and I couldn't find work. It seemed to me that there was no way out. Then I thought I'd kill myself. That way, the baby would die too. That was how miserable I was."

"And like in a movie, I heard someone call 'hello' to me. It was Alessandro. I guess I went crazy right in front of him. I cried and ranted in the comfort of his arms. Arms from home; someone who knew me when I was a child. He held me until I was calmed and then he told me what to do."

"What?" Julie was spellbound.

"He said that no baby should ever be aborted. I think . . . I think that he had just had something go wrong with his marriage . . . I'm not sure about that part, but it's a feeling I had. He had tears in his eyes, Julie. And some sadness." She squeezed Julie's hands and continued. "He gave me money. Took me to a doctor he knew. Made me eat right and helped me when Chiara was born. She was born in the first light of day and Zara was the nurse at the clinic who brought her to me so I could nurse her. We fell in love while Chiara suckled." Teodora's fine dark eyes were misty. "Some romance, huh?" She shook her head. "Two women and a little baby girl. Poor and odd. Just like in all the storybooks." Her laugh was bittersweet.

"And then Alessandro helped me again. He found us a place to stay and gave me some money so I could take care of the baby and take care of myself. Then, when Chiara was a little older, he came to tell me that my mother was dying and suggested that we come back here and run the bakery for her. He made me promise that I wouldn't tell anyone about what he'd done, and he promised me that he'd never tell anyone about how my life had been." She sniffed suddenly and two large, slow tears dropped from her face, splotching the box she held in her hand. "He said it would be better if no one ever knew and that it was only a gift of money, anyhow. But it was more than a gift of just money. It was a gift of friendship from one person who had run from Malafortuna to another. And we've both kept our promises." She wiped her face. "He saved my life, and Chiara's life and he brought me to the place where I met Zara." She snuffled. "And I think you really love him and you should know how good he is underneath." Julie's own eyes were wet. "And you must promise me now that you won't tell him that I told you." Her grin was watery, "Maybe not until after you're married to him anyway."

✦ ✦ ✦

He hoped he'd find her at home, maybe cooking in the kitchen. Whenever he couldn't help thinking of her, he envisioned her at the stove, stirring some savory mixture, her face pink-cheeked, her hair escaping it's usual neat bun, perhaps with a wisp dangling in the middle of her delectable neck. He'd dreamed of her for years and years, ever since he'd been old enough to realize that girls were made for men to love. She'd never really looked at him, not that way anyway. That kind of look had been reserved for Paolo. And so he'd turned to other women, any other woman, lots of other women. He'd risked ridicule, being called names, being laughed about. He knew they all called him a *mammoni*, a boy-man who clung to his mother. In truth, there was really no one but Marina that he'd ever wanted to be with.

His heart ached when she married. What could he have said to her? Would she have listened if he told her that Paolo would break her heart? And when Paolo did break her heart, he could only watch from the sidelines, forbidden by every rule they lived with, to ever tell her how much he loved her. If she'd ever given him one of that kind of glance, or a word that she could feel the way he did, then no rule, no taboo, no gossip, no scorn, would have kept him from her. But alas, to her, he was only a friend, good old Massimo who chased women and lived with his mother. And she was a married lady, even though the man she'd married had left her more than ten years ago.

But today, there were two telephone calls. One from Nargi, telling him that the murder investigations had been placed in the Unsolved Files. "It was the work of some lunatic thief. You can forget about it, Nulla. The case is no longer open."

The second telephone call had come from the police station in Central Rome. Paolo Corbone was dead. A heart attack, they said. Too much pressure? Too many entanglements? Or just bad genes? Massimo didn't know and didn't care. He rubbed his chin and felt the bristles. Perhaps he should shave before he went to tell her that she was a widow now.

✦ ✦ ✦

It was a perfect afternoon. They drove up the mountain, away from the road that led to Torriano. "Where are we going?"

"Nowhere. Isn't it marvelous?" He used the Italian *"meraviglioso"*, and she rolled the syllables around in her mouth. Why did everything sound so much better in Italian?

They passed a deserted old building. "What's that place, Alessandro?" She loved any excuse to say his name.

"It used to be a monastery, maybe two hundred years ago." He drove past it and then slowed down for a moment. "It's a nice old building. Look at the proportions. It could be renovated easily."

"What would you do with it?" She joked, "Make another branch of your factory here?"

He looked at the old building thoughtfully. "That's not such a bad idea. I wonder . . . " He mused, and then a hawk swooped down, nearly hitting the windshield and he braked suddenly, putting his arm across her body to keep her from sliding forward. His arm pressed against her and she could feel her heart begin to thump like a crazy thing. He slowed the car down to a crawl and reached over, kissing her hungrily. The hawk flew back into the sky, keening a mournful call, and they broke apart, laughing. He held onto her hand and she put her hand on top of his. A huge farm truck, loaded with hay and chickens, came up behind them, blowing it's horn. Alessandro laughed out loud and started the car up again. Triumphantly, he tromped on the gas and they sped away from the hawk and the farm truck and everyone and everything.

They drove up and up the mountain, spiraling around the dizzying turns and then they came to a grassy meadow. Alessandro pulled the Ferrari close to the banks of a stream that tumbled across it, the perfect place for a picnic. He spread a blue and white checked cloth on the grass and laid out a basket of food, big square napkins, shining green glass goblets and some silverware. He took two bottles of wine out of the trunk of the car and laid them between two rocks in the stream so that the ice cold water would chill them.

They split the crusty bread that she had made that morning with his pocketknife and drizzled olive oil over the pieces. They cut slices of *soprasotta* and creamy goat cheese and forgot to use the knives and forks. The sun beat down on their heads and Julie shrugged off the light sweater she wore over her yellow polo shirt.

Alessandro lay on his side on the blanket and propped himself up on his elbow. "Tell me about your divorce, Julie. What happened?" She looked at him, her hand halfway to her mouth, then bit at the piece of bread and chewed for a moment.

"I thought he was wonderful. I'd known him since I was a child. He was a few years older than I, a friend of one of my cousins. He'd always been popular, out of my reach." She held out her glass and he poured her some wine. "Then, one day, he started to pay attention to me, courted me off my feet and we were married. I thought I was the happiest girl alive."

"And?"

"And I was, for two days."

"Two days?"

"Two days." She nodded firmly, looking out towards the tops of the hills in the distance. "I found out that he had gone upstairs at the wedding reception, maybe an hour after we exchanged vows. He'd gone up with one of the wedding guests, the wife of one of his clients. They'd made love, right on top of the guests' coats on my mother and father's bed. She told me, right to my face, laughing at my innocence. And then she told me that they had done it the night before the wedding, too." She drank a little of the wine and deliberately didn't look down on him.

"I confronted him, and he laughed at me too. He said I'd better be grown up about it. He told me he was too much of a man to be tied down to one woman. To quit my sniveling and put on a good face." Alessandro touched her hand gently and she couldn't help smiling down at him. "It seems so long ago. I was devastated then. I didn't know what to do. There was no one I could tell. I was ashamed, felt it was my fault. That if I'd been prettier, or smarter, or more sophisticated, I could have held him. Now, of course, I know better, but I was only a young girl, and he was my only love."

Alessandro's face was thunderous and Julie turned his hand over in hers. "It's over. Long over." She patted his hand.

"The bastard," Alessandro muttered and Julie nodded.

"He really was. And I thought I could change him." She sighed and swallowed the rest of her glass. She held it out and he rolled over and poured her another glass. "I tried everything. I cut my hair, went to beauty parlors, tried new perfumes, read books on how to please your man in bed. And I did, please him in bed, that is. But it still didn't keep him home. He cheated on me left and right, having affairs with his secretary, his clients, the *wives* of his clients. He was so charming, so successful and everyone--including my mother and father--thought that we were the ideal couple." She sighed deeply. "And then I thought that if I had a baby, he might change. So I tried a little more, hoping to make a family. If I had a baby to love, maybe I wouldn't have minded about him so much. That's how idealistic I was. Silly little me." Her voice changed and became a little huskier. "And then one of his old girlfriends told me . . . She said . . . She said I was a nice person and too good to be married to him. She told me he . . . he would never father any children. That he'd . . . he'd had a vasectomy a year before we married. That he never wanted any babies to mess up his life and that he'd make sure that he never would." Her voice ran down. "That was the end for me. I filed for divorce the next morning and never saw him again. I understand he's married again and lives in Philadelphia." She shrugged. "So I went to school in New York and tried to make some sort of life for myself.

His arms enfolded her and he rocked her back and forth. She clutched him tightly, but her eyes were dry. "Do you still love him?" He couldn't help but ask. "Do you?"

"I loved him for a long time after I found out what he was like. I'd loved him for so long, I didn't know how to un-love him. But I didn't *like* him. And I told myself every day, that I didn't love him any more. And then, one day, it was true. I didn't love him at all."

He cradled her and kissed her forehead. "I'm sorry." He whispered and she turned her head and kissed his mouth. The wine bottle tipped over, running its ruby wetness over the edge of the blue and white cloth, but neither of them noticed it at all.

❖ ❖ ❖

Marina gasped and her knees buckled. Massimo grabbed at her and held her, "I'm sorry, Marina. He was a bastard, but I know you loved him." She began to cry and he patted her on the back, helpless to know what to say. She sniffled and rubbed her face into his shirt and he wanted to kiss her tears away. She said something, muffled in the clean white linen of his chest. "What?" He asked. "What did you say?"

She pulled her head back and he saw that her eyes were puffy with tears. Her lips wobbled and he drowned in her beauty, wanting nothing more than to make her happy. She tried on a watery smile. "I said, 'I'm so glad that he's dead'." He blinked, not comprehending.

"I've hated him for more than twelve years, Massimo. He made me so unhappy when he was here, and he's made me and Anton unhappy since he's been gone." She pulled back a little more and he reluctantly loosened his grip on her. "I hope he didn't have any pain. I hope he died quickly, but, thank God that Anton and I are free from him." She sucked in her breath and let it out in a long sigh, broke away from his arms and went over to the stove. "I need a drink or some coffee. How about you?" And he watched her from behind, her neat, shining hair a little disarranged, with one wisp hanging down the middle of her delectable neck. "Can you tell Anton?" She asked as she turned around and saw him watching her.

"*Me?* You want *me* to tell him?" She nodded. "Why me?" She shrugged. She couldn't tell him that she was afraid to tell her son.

"It might be better if he heard it from another man."

He couldn't refuse her anything. Not even this. How the hell was he going to tell the boy his father was dead? He looked at her pretty pink cheeks and didn't dare think of the future. He patted her shoulder awkwardly, wanting to sweep her into his arms. Instead, he smiled lopsidedly, and told her that he'd find Anton and tell him.

He loitered outside the schoolyard until he saw Anton loping toward home. "Let's walk, son." Anton looked up at him, alarmed. "I have to tell you about your father . . . ."

The boy wept, his gangly half-boy's, half-man's length cradled in Massimo's arms. "I'm *glad* he's dead, Massimo." Anton spit out the words fiercely. Massimo hugged him, feeling the bones and smelling the smell of a young boy. He rocked Anton back and forth, his own heart nearly breaking.

If only this were his own son. If only . . . . Then Anton sighed mightily and Massimo patted him, keeping his arm around Anton's shoulder. "Is my mother all right?" Massimo nodded, unable to speak. "Good." Anton snuffled a few times. "I'm ashamed that I cried."

"Are you *crazy*, Anton." Massimo punched him lightly on his shoulder. "He was your father and sometimes even a man has to shed a few tears."

"He was a real son-of-a-bitch, huh?" The boy's laugh was unsteady and he wiped his shirtsleeve across his nose. "He made Mamma so unhappy."

"I cried for your mother's grief many times. I could have killed your father for causing her to cry. " Massimo's voice was low.

"You could have?"

"I could have. But I had no right to. You understand, son?"

"Not really, but it makes me feel better." He knuckled his eyes dry and they walked back, arm in arm.

"Hey, Massimo? " Anton's awkward boy's body bumped against him. "Can I try to find the evidence at Otto's house? Just you and me will know what I'm doing."

"Julie will rip us to pieces. "

"It will be our secret. Just us men." Anton's chest swelled visibly. Massimo rubbed his chin.

"Come on, Massimo." Anton danced in front of him. Massimo laughed. The boy seemed to be over his grief. How fast they forget when they're thirteen years old!

"I'll think about it." If he could get some evidence, Nargi would look like a fool. And somewhere in Otto's house, if Otto was the cousin . . . if they were lucky . . . he was sure, was the wedding ring and some kind of a necklace. If Anton could find them, he could solve the whole case and then maybe Marina would see him in a new light. He'd have to be awfully careful, though, and be sure Anton was well protected. "We'll talk later." Massimo wagged his finger in Anton's face. "But don't try anything until we've made up a good plan."

"When I was a kid, Massimo," Anton's head was nearly at Massimo's shoulder. "I used to dream that my father had died." Massimo smiled gently. "Then," the boy ducked his head shyly, "I'd dream that my mother married you."

"*Me?*"

"Yeah. He was a deserter. You're a policeman. Someone that any boy would look up to." Anton was blushing. "It was a silly dream, I know, but I always wished I had a father like you. A policeman! You must think I'm a ninny, don't you?"

"No, Anton. I think that's the nicest compliment I've ever had. I'd be proud to have a son like you." If only you knew, lad. If only you knew how I feel.

"You have so many women, Massimo." He felt brave enough to speak to Massimo, man to man. "How come you never married?"

"An interesting question, Anton. One that deserves a lot of thought." In his own embarrassment, Massimo thumped Anton on his back, nearly knocking the boy over. He'd never realized how is womanizing might look to the boys in the village. "Let's you and me get your mother and the three of us can go out for supper tonight. Your mother deserves a night out, don't you think?"

✦ ✦ ✦

He kissed her neck, he kissed her mouth, he kissed her ears and the little spot under the angle of her chin where the bone stuck out and a little hollow beckoned--she was drugged with his lips, but that's all he did. He didn't touch her, or try to move his body against her, or anything more. And it was stupendous. Like being fifteen again and necking in the back seat of a car. Lips only; nothing else. It was more than exciting. It was wonderful.

And what was wrong with him? Why wasn't he trying anything else? She pulled back and opened her eyes. He was watching her through the waterfall of his lashes, and there was a little smile on his lips. They looked at each other, their faces inches away. "And you, Alessandro." Ah, how she loved to say his name. "It's your turn for true confessions. Tell me about your marriage and what happened, Alessandro."

He rolled over on his back and settled his arms underneath his head. "I knew I'd get asked." He crossed his legs and it was all she could do to not throw herself on top of him. "The story makes me look like a fool." He made a funny noise in his throat, "But then, I generally look like a fool in front of you anyway." She rolled her eyes at him. Silly man!

"The business was becoming very successful. I was working like a dog, trying to make it all come together--financing, sales-- I was doing everything myself. Renata's father was one of the bankers who put up a lot of money. It was one of those crucial times--I needed the financing and I needed it then. He introduced me to her. She was young and lovely." Julie hated her.

"Her father let me know that he'd like it if we married. He implied that the financing and Renata were tied up in one little package. I didn't love her, not really, but it could have been worse. We courted, while I tried to figure out what to do." He uncrossed his arms and propped himself up. "I know when I tell it that it makes me seem like a crass idiot, but, honestly, Julie, *I* was the one being manipulated, not her. She told me that she was pregnant." Julie gasped and drew back. "And that seemed to make the decision easy for me. I was delighted. I always wanted a family and well, why not her? We were well suited and her father made the loan available to Alessi Limited."

"We were married in a very quiet, very elegant ceremony. Only our parents and our immediate families. My mother was happy I was married. She never got on very well with Renata, but, well, she never said anything or interfered. Renata's father was happy. Renata seemed happy, and I--well, I was pleased." His voice trailed off and she watched him as he looked out over the hills.

"She changed almost overnight. From a nice, pleasant new wife to a shrew. I put it down to her pregnancy and tried everything I could think of to make her happy. I'd maybe be able to do things differently now, but I was still young and inexperienced. I didn't know how to handle the situation well. Alessi Limited was doing well. I was smart in business, but not so smart in my personal life. I thought I could make her happy. I did what she asked me to do. I bought her clothes, jewels, we went on vacations, a new car. Nothing was enough. She spent millions and millions of *lire*. It was like she was punishing me and I didn't understand why. Every day was a crisis, screaming, throwing things, tantrums. And then she started to see other men. Anyone, the doorman, a taxicab driver, some man she saw in a restaurant, anyone. I'd come home and find signs that she brought them home. I think she wanted me to know. Every moment, she sulked, pouted, screamed and finally went home to her father."

"Maybe I could have done more. I don't know." He shrugged. "I just couldn't make it work. I even tried to get her to see a doctor. I thought maybe she was sick, needed help . . . Her father tried, too. He never blamed me for anything. But there wasn't anything either of us could do. It was as if she was inhabited by a devil."

"And the baby?" She didn't look at him, but she had to know.

"The baby," His voice was bleak. "She told me that she didn't want to have any children. She had it aborted the week before the wedding." The silence seemed to go on for a long time. "She never said anything to me then, She let me think that the baby was still coming until after all the trouble started. Her father -- poor man. He was broken hearted. He lost his grandchild, me, a man that he respected, and his daughter. From then on, she drifted from man to man, never satisfied. She's . . . Sometimes I hear about her. She's in France now, I think."

She didn't know what to say. He paused for a few moments and then continued in a matter-of-fact voice, "Her father's company still invests with us. Alessi has done very well, and his original investment has multiplied a thousand times over for them. He's always polite to me, even pleasant. But he's a broken man over Renata." He shook his head. "I don't understand, even now."

They sat together with their thoughts as the sun slowly moved down to the tops of the mountains. Then he slapped her gently on her thigh. "A couple of romantic flops we are, no?"

She looked at him and laughed ruefully, *"Veramente,* Alessandro."

He stood up and pulled her to her feet. "Maybe we both need to try again." He kept hold of her hand and brought it to his lips. She couldn't breathe. "Maybe."

They drove home, each with his own thoughts, each hoping that perhaps this time . . . Each crazy in love with the other.

"You know more about my family than even I do, now that you've gotten all the gossip in the village." He drove casually, one hand on the wheel. With the other, he covered her own hand and she could feel the heat from him. "But I don't know too much about you. Tell me about your family, your mother, your father -- everything."

She waited to see if he would keep talking, but he only glanced inquiringly at her. She grinned inwardly. He was ever so much better than Roger from California. "Well, as you know, I was born in Connecticut . . . "

She told him everything she could think of. He listened, obviously interested, and asked a lot of questions, especially about her brother, Moe. "I always wanted a brother. Renzo and I, we were always close when we were children; almost like brothers." And he told her about his childhood, funny stories, and she imagined the sturdy, black-haired ruffian who had been the smartest boy in the entire village.

"And other than your beauty, *Carissima,* " he teased her, "What should a man who might . . . well . . . you know, be interested in you," She sneaked a glance and saw that he was actually blushing, *blushing!* "What should this man also know about you?" There, he finally got it all out!

"Hmmmm," it was her turn to feel uncomfortable. "He'd have to know that I have a horrible temper, that I can get very angry." She thought for a moment. "And I'm rather romantic. I'm a great cook. I hate phoniness and pretense. Money doesn't matter much to me, but I think I like nice things too. I'm stubborn and opinionated . . . and, well, I've been told that I'm a fantastic dancer."

His laughter bellowed out. "And do you really want a big family?" He sneaked another look at her flustered face.

"Yes, Alessandro. I want a big family." They drove for a mile or more in silence. "And you?"

"I'd be a happy man if I had three more *bambini* than Renzo and Carmella." He winked audaciously at her. "And all of them with red hair!"

CHAPTER ELEVEN

He decided not to go to school that morning. He deserved a day to himself, after all, hadn't his father just died? Usually, when someone's family had a death, the person stayed out of school for at least a few days. There was usually a big funeral, and a procession following the coffin to the cemetery. This kind of death, where he never even knew what his father looked like, this kind was a little different, though. Perhaps he should be grieving. Ha! For what? He didn't even know what his father *looked* like. Why should he grieve? He told himself stoutly, he was glad, *glad,* that his father was dead. But down in the vicinity of where his soul rested, there seemed to be a lump of unhappiness.

He didn't say anything to his mother, nor did he say anything to Julie about missing school. It was probably better that the two of them think that he'd gone as usual. Both of them were a little odd at breakfast, come to think of it. No word was mentioned at all about the death. Nothing at all.

Last night, Massimo had escorted his mother and himself to La Famiglia Ristorante for dinner. It should have been pleasant, after all, they were comfortable with one another, but . . . it had been an uncomfortable time. None of them said much of anything to each other, except mundane things like "pass the bread, please." All around them there was buzzing, everyone speculating about his father's death, and everyone wondering why Massimo was with them. Anton had been hungry, and eaten a large plate of *calamari fritte,* followed by a salad and *zuppa inglese* for dessert. Massimo had only toyed with his food, and his mother had barely eaten a thing.

He was exhausted when they got home, and he said goodnight to both of them. Massimo had taken off his jacket and seated himself at the kitchen table. His mother was at the stove, preparing coffee, and Anton had kissed her on the cheek, telling her goodnight. She had turned and hugged him hard, and then he went to bed. He thought his dreams might have been bad ones, after all, it *was* his father who had died, but, no, he'd fallen into a deep, dreamless sleep the moment his head hit the pillow.

Chiara had looked at him with deep sad eyes when he picked up the morning bread at the bakery. Teodora had come over and touched his hand. "We're sorry to hear about your father, Anton." Chiara waited until Teodora went back to the ovens and then told Anton that she would talk with him after school.

As he left the bakery, Zara called him and came running after him with a large white box tied with string. "Here," she thrust the box into his arms, "Take this for your mother from us."

He gave the box to Marina. It was a chestnut cream-stuffed *pandoro*, and he was so ravenous at breakfast that he'd nearly eaten the whole thing.

And when he left the house, his mother was still sitting at the table. Her eyes looked tired, and she was making a circular pattern on the tablecloth with the tip of her spoon. Julie had seemed preoccupied, and he heard that she was going to Milano with Zio Alessandro. They were going to the opera and wouldn't be back until tomorrow. "Have a good time at the opera, Julie." She nodded, brightening, and Anton kissed them both on their cheeks before he went out the door.

And now, he walked along the road to Zio Nunzio's farm, damned if he was going to stay cooped up in school today. He picked up a stick and stabbed at several trees along the way. "Ha! Take that!" he jousted, poking the stick so hard that it snapped in two. He picked up another stick, a stronger one this time, and managed to knock down two apples from one of Zio's trees. He put the apples in his pocket to munch on later, when he was hungry again.

"Is there anything I can do for you before we leave?" Julie was a little worried.

Marina looked so exhausted. Even though she'd hated Paolo, this must be an emotional time for her.

"No, *Cara,* I'm fine. Just a little tired." Marina touched Julie's hand.

"Are you sure? I don't have to go to Milano . . . ."

"Don't be silly. You'll have such a wonderful time at the opera." Marina patted Julie's hand with finality. *"Gianni Schicchi* is one of the funniest ones I've ever seen."

"I saw it when I was eleven years old," Julie told her. My Grandmother Antonina--except I was supposed to think she was my great-aunt--was a famous opera star in her day and she took me as a treat. I remember the stupendous curtain and the huge chandeliers, and I remember that she took me out for chocolate ice cream afterwards. I think I was much too young to enjoy the plot. All I can remember is *"O mio babbino caro."*

"Your grandmother pretended to be your great-aunt?" All traces of weariness was wiped off Marina's face. "What happened?" She never tired of hearing about Julie's family.

"She was a pip, so I understand. I never knew until I was much older that she was really my father's mother. I mean, my father was brought up by her brother, Rafaelo." She laughed at Marina's perplexed face. "Wait!" Julie put her hand up. "I have to tell it from the beginning."

"There were six children born to my great-great grandmother Francesca. The oldest was Antonina. Rafael and Michele were born next and they were twins. Anyway, Antonina's father was the Count, Anton del Guidice, *not* Carlo Rosato, who was the man Francesca was married to." Marina's eyes almost crossed as she tried to follow the complexities of Julie's family tree.

"Antonina became a famous diva, and she had a secret affair. She couldn't bring the baby up normally because she was always on stage or traipsing around with the opera company, so she gave the baby, whom she named Anton after her *real* father, the Count, to her brother Rafe to bring up. Rafe married my aunt Giulietta Fiorile, Sal's daughter, so both my father AND my grandmother were illegitimate! See?"

"Not really." Marina's voice was faint.

"Here," Julie said kindly, "let me show you," and she drew a chart on the back of a paper napkin. "See? Now you can understand how there are so many Antons and Antoninas in my background."

Marina gazed at the chart and nodded her head dubiously and Julie laughed out loud.

The unfortunate death of Paolo Carbone receded a little with the diversion of Julie's confusing family story. "I can study this and try to make some sense of it when I have nothing to do." Marina turned the paper upside down "It looks just as sensible this way up! Oh, Julie! Thank God you are here!

How could I have survived all this without you? " She began to laugh. "I think, for myself, I'll have a nice quiet day. After all, I have to get used to being a widow!"

✦✦✦

Massimo spent the morning pacing up and down under the grape arbor. Nonna Graziella watched him, her bottom lip protruding thoughtfully. Something was the matter. The boy had barely eaten his breakfast this morning.

The police telephone line rang out, shrilling in the morning air, and Massimo grabbed it, grateful for something to do. It was Vincenza Talerico. Umberto had gone on one of his drunken rages again. The *bastardo* had ripped the gold chain off her neck, nearly decapitating her! *This* time she was going to have him arrested! *This* time she wouldn't change her mind! Massimo told her to lie down and put a cold cloth on her neck. He'd make the three hour drive out to their farm in the mountains later that afternoon to write out her complaint. "And this time, you'd better make sure you put him in jail! If I drive all the way out there and you've changed your mind again, Vincenza, I'm going to arrest you!" Vincenza screeched out her agreement.

He hung up the phone and rubbed his hands gleefully together. "Nonna! Where are you? I'm going out to Talerico's farm to arrest Umberto once and for all!" He jumped into his car and drove off.

"You're wasting your time!" Nonna Graziella yelled after him, shaking her fist at the departing car, "She'll never have him arrested! Never!"

✦✦✦

Julie packed. She really only had one elaborate dress with her, a white sheath, slitted at the side nearly to her hip. The bodice was high in the front, very chaste and modest, then dipped daringly almost to her waist in back. It was sexy and yet innocent. "Just like me!" She grinned at her reflection in the little mirror. With it, she wore a beaded shawl, dark blue with even darker blue sequins and sparkles. Very retro. She swirled the shawl around her shoulders, dipping and dancing, watching her reflection go in and out of the mirror. She slipped everything off and folded the dress and shawl into her suitcase. Other than pantyhose, there was nothing else to be worn under the dress. She looked into the mirror and exulted in the wicked gleam in her own eyes.

And there was this nightgown. A wisp of pale peach froth with two tiny straps that fell down at the slightest movement. Very elegant, very understated. Very sexy. She smiled serenely and folded it under the dress as the telephone rang downstairs in Marina's apartment. It rang and rang. Marina must be out. She rushed down the steps to answer it.

"Moe!" She was overjoyed to hear his voice. He wanted to know how the investigation was progressing. "Nothing, yet." She was dismayed that since yesterday, she hadn't thought at all about the murders. "I've been with Alessandro, Moe . . . and we're going to the opera tonight in Milano."

"What are you going to see?" Moe was an opera nut, too. Everyone in her family was potty about operas.

"*Gianni Schicchi.*"

"I remember that one. It has '*O Mio Babbino Caro*'," he sang the title in a surprisingly good voice. "Right?"

"Uh huh. Where the guy pretends to be the dead man, and all the relatives want the dead man's money. I went to see it with Antonina once when I was a kid."

"Enjoy it and tell me how it was. I envy you. *La Scala* is supposed to be so beautiful. Maybe Blanchie and I will come to Milan on our honeymoon."

"When are you getting married?"

"Who knows." Moe shifted his shoulders guiltily. They really should make some definite plans. He changed the subject adroitly, "So tell me about Alessandro. You have this lilt in your voice, Jul. Is this guy the one, honey babe?" Moe adored his sister. There was nothing he'd like better than to see her married to some nice guy, bouncing fat babies on her knees. "Is he good enough for you?"

"Maybe, Moe." Her voice was shaky. "I didn't think so at first, but he grows on you." Her laugh was tremulous and Moe felt his heart turn over. Julie deserved a prince. A king. "I think it could be the real thing."

"Does he treat you right? In every way, Jul?" Moe's concern came right through the receiver. "No philandering? No hurting you? You don't need any more grief like last time."

"So far, so good, Moe." He could hear the gladness in her voice. "Tonight could be a big night."

"You tell him from me, he'd better watch out if he hurts you, Julie. I'll come over there and make his head fall off."

"I think everything will be fine, Moe. He's the one who found the bodies with me. On top of the mountain. He's . . . well, he's very special. I think you'd like him." Julie grinned into the phone. "And once I get back, I'm going to figure out how to search for the evidence. Oh!" She gasped suddenly.

"What?"

"The dress I'm wearing tonight! It's from Fancy's!"

"It's an omen, Julie." Julie grinned into her side of the telephone. Moe and she shared the same superstition about omens, and this one about Fancy's was electric with possibilities. But Moe was talking . . . . "Don't worry, you'll catch him yet. Now, you have a great time tonight with . . . What's his name again?"

"Alessandro. Alessandro Alessi."

"Nice name, Julie. I love you, honey."

"I love you too, Moe. Give my best to Blanche and Mom and Dad and everyone. Tell them all that I miss them."

"But that you're stayin' right there until, um, this Alessandro fish is properly netted, huh?"

"Now, Moe," her tone was prim. "You know I have to finish my book."

His strong laugh rang. "Some book. Is it a cookbook or a romance you're writing?"

"Both." She said, as she hung up the phone. "Bye, Moe."

"Bye, Julie. Good luck."

✦ ✦ ✦

When she got back from the grocery, Julie and Alessandro had already left for Milano. The house was empty, and she put the food away slowly, feeling restless and bored. She didn't *feel* like a widow, that was the problem. She could hardly remember what Paolo looked like and, as for grieving, well, how could she grieve for him? She looked at the telephone. Should she call Massimo and apologize? Poor Massimo had tried to cheer her up, but she'd been less than good company last night. Maybe he would want to have dinner here tonight. It was the least she could do for his kindness. She called but Nonna Graziella told her that he'd been called away on police business.

"It's Vincenza Talerico again." Nonna told her. Marina nodded into the telephone. Everyone in the village knew about the Talerico spats. "He says she's finally going to arrest him!"

"That will be the day."

"I'll tell him you called." Nonna's voice held a curious note. "And I send you my condolences on Paolo's death."

"Thank you, Nonna. I don't quite know how to feel about it." Marina's voice was shaky. "After all, it was more than eleven years since Paolo left me and Anton. I barely remember what it was like to be married to him."

"All the more reason to get on with your life." Marina was surprised to hear Nonna Graziella speak to her like this. "Live a little, Marina, *Carissima*. Forget the past and make a good future for yourself. You're a young woman yet. Find a good man and make him happy." She cackled loudly, "Maybe somebody local." She hung up and Marina replaced the receiver thoughtfully.

✦ ✦ ✦

The glory of a day without school began to pale. There wasn't anyone to enjoy it with and Anton was almost sorry that he wasn't in the schoolyard with his friends. Bored with his freedom, he trudged toward home. At least he could see Chiara after school and find out what homework he'd missed. His face brightened and he began to walk a little faster. He pulled one of the apples out of his jacket and reached into his pocket for the little knife he always carried. He sliced the apple and careless of what he was doing, cut the tip of his finger. "Oww!" He stuck his finger into his mouth. The taste of the blood made him think of the murders.

His steps slowed again. Why not? Massimo and Julie would *kill* him if he went ahead with the plan to catch Otto. But why not? He sucked at his cut. He was free as a bird today. He'd be careful. He could simply start the process moving that's all. He wouldn't be in any danger. Not today. He'd only mess up Otto's stuff, not do anything to get himself in real trouble. Grinning, his steps quickened again as he headed for the village square.

CHAPTER TWELVE

He'd done a great job of it. Otto's garden was a mess. The flowerpots were overturned and broken. The herbs had been ripped out of their pots. He'd hurled a brick through Otto's kitchen window, then reached through a ripped the sagging curtains off their rods. He was in the process of rocking the big glass globe back and forth on its pinnacle when he heard Otto's roar of rage. He gulped, frightened despite his bravado. Please God, don't let him kill me right off! And just as Otto came outside, raging purple with fury, he toppled the globe off. They both watched in horror as it smashed on the terrace into a million shards of mirrored glass.

"You little bastard! I'll kill you!" Otto's hands reached out for his throat. Anton goggled in fear. Otto was bigger than he'd remembered. Fatter and cruder and much more frightening. Perhaps he had gone too far. With a cry, Otto grabbed for him. He twisted free and ran away. Otto chased him down the street, yelling and screaming and Anton never ran as fast as he did that day. He hid behind the wall at the school yard, waiting for Otto to go to Massimo to complain. His heart was thudding out of his chest. Otto was obviously berserk, his face purple with uncontrolled rage. Anton hoped he wouldn't have a heart attack! At least, not before they were able to get the evidence!

✦ ✦ ✦

They changed for the opera at Alessandro's condominium, he in his bedroom and she in one of the guest rooms. She felt stiff and silly, dressing on one side of the place while he was in his room. Alessandro had given her a melting look when he showed her the guest bedroom. Perhaps it was some kind of a test. Perhaps it was better that they dressed separately, otherwise, they might be unable to get to see *Gianni Schicchi.* She slid the white dress on and looked at her reflection in the long pier mirror set on the floor. She looked good. He'd be pleased.

She puffed on a little of the vanilla spice perfume her cousin Annie made just for her. A little dab here, a little dab there. Her cinnamon hair was freshly washed and slid around her face in a silky curtain. She adjusted the scarf around her shoulders so that it settled in satiny folds, hiding the disappearing back of the dress. She'd keep it like this—demure--until they got to *La Scala.* She was excited, keyed-up, going to the beautiful old opera house that her grandmother, her *real* grandmother, had sung in.

She stuck her head out. He was still in his room. Glory be! It certainly was a beautiful condominium. She pulled her head back in and snooped around the guest room. She poked into the medicine cabinet. Lots of female beauty preparations, lined up on the shelves, awaiting the next lady guest, but all of them unopened. Was Alessandro smart, or did he merely have good housekeeping services? The linen, brand new on the bed, had a pattern of violets against a light blue background. Again, she wondered, how many women had been up here, primping to go out?

"Are you ready?" He called. She jumped back, afraid that she'd been caught being nosey, but he was in the salon.

"Ready." She glided out. In her silver sling back pumps, she was nearly as tall as he was, and he gaped at her in delighted admiration.

"You look like a queen." He took her hand in his. "Beautiful." He leaned forward and kissed her gently on the lips. "And I'll be a good king and not mess up your make-up." He winked at her. "Yet". She dimpled at him and wondered if he knew that if he kissed her again, she'd tear off the tuxedo that he wore. He looked that marvelous. *Meraviglioso,* she amended herself.

They were slightly uncomfortable with each other on the elevator ride down, muttering inane remarks. "It is a lovely building."

"Yes. These elevators, sometimes it takes a few minutes to get one."

"Is *La Scala* far from here?"

"Not too far. It's a beautiful night, no?"

"Mmmmm. This is such a lovely building."

He'd ordered a limousine and she felt like Cinderella being handed into its capacious, luxurious back. There was a freshly opened bottle of champagne cooling in a silver urn and there were two crystal glasses on a silver tray.

"I feel like a rich princess. Do you go whole hog every time you take someone to the opera?"

"Whole hog?"

"American slang. It means 'pulling all the stops out'". He still looked faintly puzzled, "Um, ah, doing everything possible, lighting *all* the lights, spending as much money as you can, doing *every*thing."

"Ah," he said. "Yes, the full hog. Not for everyone." He gestured to her with the champagne. "Yes?"

"*Certamante!*" She sipped the golden liquid and thought that maybe having a ton of money wasn't such a bad thing after all.

Their driver pulled the long car smoothly to the front steps. Julie was glad to see that Alessandro opened his own door and, motioning to the driver, opened hers too. He held out his arm and she alighted, feeling just lovely.

La Scala was lit like some great jewel, blazing with lights, sconces, chandeliers, and flickering dazzles. They were immediately met by a uniformed majordomo, who bowed to Alessandro and led them inside. They went into the foyer. Julie was suffused with astonishment as she saw marble pillars and columns, carved with cherubs and cherubini, stunning frescos and huge paintings hung with gold frames. "It's marvelous!" She said. "*Meraviglioso!*" They didn't go up the famed staircase, but were whisked through a small door into a private hall and then into a jewel box of an elevator that brought them straight to their balcony box. Julie's mouth was open in delight, and Alessandro had to hold himself in check from grabbing her and kissing her silly in front of their escort. The man held the door of their box open and Alessandro deftly slipped him the best tip he'd make in a month. The man smiled, genuinely pleased, and shut the door, cocooning them together. Alessandro turned to her and took her elbows. *Now* he kissed her mouth. And kissed it again. And still one more time, this time, unable to keep his hands from gripping her face on either side. "*Carissima*," he said shakily.

She gulped audibly, "Oh, Alessandro," and she kissed him back, one time, elemental and fierce, with her hands clutched around the bands of hardness that were his upper arms. Their eyes were level and she could see the flames of the great chandelier reflected in the depths of his dark pupils. He looked at her for a long moment, and only a nerve jumping at the side of his jaw let her know the passion in him.

The audience erupted into applause, signaling the entrance of the orchestra. The noise broke their spell. "Later, *Cara*, I will wait for later." He motioned for her to sit down. She grinned at him and regally swept her satin stole off, allowing him the first glimpse of her naked back. His swift, indrawn gasp was reward enough for her. She sat, back straight, like a queen, for an instant, then, whooped delightedly as she nearly hung over the balcony to look at the stage below. Alessandro gripped her hand and she was as happy as it was possible to be.

Kendra saw them the moment they came into the box. She saw the kisses, could feel the intensity, even from where she sat. She gritted her teeth like a dog and the beautiful line of her jaw was spoiled when she drew back her lips in anger. "*Putana*!" She spit out. So *this* was why Alessandro had been that way! Her date leaped to his feet, clapping as the curtain opened, but Kendra only sat, vindictive and furious. How *dare* he show such public affection to that woman? And who the hell *was* she?

The opera unfolded before them. "Gianni Schicchi was evidently a real person," Alessandro whispered. "He lived hundreds of years ago and actually was supposed to have pulled off a swindle just like this one."

"Trust an Italian to think this up!"

"And the penalty for falsifying a Will in the 13th Century was cutting off one's hand and banishment."

"Yow!" She said as the music swirled around her.

Kendra's brain churned furiously. She suddenly thought of the key that she had surreptitiously made several weeks ago. She excused herself, pleading a sudden headache, and left her escort to enjoy the rest of the performance. "I'll be back in a half hour after I get some medicine. No, no. You stay here. I'll go and return before you'll even notice." She almost ran up the corridor.

Outside *La Scala*, she quickly hailed a taxicab and directed him to drive to her apartment. "Wait here!" She ordered and the driver blew a kiss to her. A *bellissima* lady like her, he'd go to the moon , if she but asked. Kendra clawed through her top drawer and found the key. Thank goodness she'd had it made last month when she'd had the opportunity. Alessandro would have strangled her if he knew. "*Stronzo*!" she spit out. She'd fix his ass. She stood for a moment. What the hell could she do?   She prowled around, seeking inspiration and saw the red nightdress with the frou-frou neck and the red high-heeled shoes. The things she'd bought especially for Alessandro. "Well, he'll get them in a different way!"   She got back in the taxi and ordered him to drive to the front of Alessandro's condominium building.

"Wait here," she told the driver. "I'll be ten or fifteen minutes."

"Like before, I'll wait for a beauty like you forever," the driver promised, watching her rear end in its tight dress run up to the front door.

She let herself in carefully. There was no one there. She saw the clothes in the guest bedroom and sneered. And then she saw the wispy peach nightdress. She grabbed it, intending to rip it into a thousand pieces. Instead, she made herself think of the best way to accomplish her revenge. She found a sheet of paper and wrote . . . .

She was back at the opera house just before the curtain. "Feeling better?" Her date asked.

"Much, much better, darling. You can't know how much better I feel," she told him, putting her long-nailed hand high up on his thigh.

✦ ✦ ✦

Marina went crazy when she heard about the damage. She hauled him out of his room and slapped his face. "Why, Anton? Why?" She cried, ineffectually punching at his chest in complete frustration. He gulped and stood still, letting her pound at him, feeling like a complete worm to hurt his mother like this. And he couldn't explain anything to her. Not yet. Not until they had the evidence. And where was Massimo to help him?

"He should be horsewhipped in the village square!" Otto menaced. "Struck with a whip until he bleeds," he spat contemptuously on Marina's kitchen floor.

She whirled at Otto angrily. "Mind your manners, you pig! I don't excuse what my son has done. It's . . . it's . . . *Inexcusable!*" She sucked in a deep breath and shuddered it out. "but that is no excuse for you to act like an animal too." Anton felt like a snake. But what could he do? He just *couldn't* say anything in his defense now. He bit at his lip, trying not to cry. Big policemen didn't cry when they were sent into the line of duty. He snuffled and brushed a tear away as Marina sighed and spoke to Otto. "I apologize, Signor Zampone. I am shamed by my son's behavior." Anton wanted to run to Marina's arms and tell her everything. But he stood stock-still, cowed and embarrassed. Marina pushed him contemptuously and Otto's fat mouth curled in a sneer. He was enjoying Anton's distress enormously. Anton hoped with all his heart to see Otto hanged for what he'd done. "He'll work for you, Signore. For three weeks. For free, of course, until he has repaired all that he has damaged." Despite his fear and shame, a song sang in Anton's heart. Just what they had planned! Otto nodded, grudgingly, and almost made a move to hit Anton. Marina slid in between them. "You must promise me that you won't strike him, though," Otto's face made a surly nod. Marina turned again and slapped Anton hard. "That punishment, Signor Zampone, I will reserve for myself." She glared at Anton and motioned him to go to his room. "There's no school tomorrow. He will be at your house first thing tomorrow, Signore. Ready to do whatever you need him to do."

Alone in the darkness of his room, Anton moaned in frustration. It hadn't gone quite the way he'd expected. If only Massimo had been there! If only he could tell his mother just what he was trying to accomplish. There was a knock on the back door. Massimo? No. He could hear Chiara in the kitchen, asking for him, and then he heard his mother's brief excuse for him. The heat of shame curled around him, even though he'd accomplished exactly what he'd set out to. He sniffed back the tears and stuck out his lip in defiance. Just wait until they all found out that he'd helped to catch a murderer! Just wait! They'd all feel bad that they'd yelled at him, even his mother! He pushed his head under the covers so she couldn't hear him and cried himself to sleep.

❖ ❖ ❖

And on the lonely road back from the Talerico's house, Massimo kicked frustratingly at the flat tire of his car. It was nearly dark and it would be suicide to try to walk anywhere but back to the Talerico's farm in the inky night. Once again, he tried to use his cell phone, to call Mamma or Marina to let them know where he was, but the high peaks of the mountain range rendered it inoperable.

❖ ❖ ❖

They left the opera hall in a daze of love, holding onto one another's hands as if they'd never let go. He pulled her close in the limousine and, when he thought the driver was preoccupied, showered her neck with tiny kisses.

The driver smiled to himself. Signor Alessi was a nice man and the two of them seemed crazy about one another. He hoped they'd be happy. He pocketed the huge tip and bid them good night at the front of the condominium.

It was a different situation this time in the elevator. No platitudes, no discussions about the weather. Only burning kisses and the promise of the night to come. He scooped her up as the elevator doors opened and carried her down the hall to his alcove. Holding her, giggling into his neck, he managed to open the door and then he put her down on the sofa. He closed the door and dropped to his knees beside her. "You have to know how I feel, *Carissima.*"

Carissima. Such a word. My darling darling. Alessandro, my love. The words boomed in her head. She was amazed that she hadn't shouted them out. . She held his head in her hands and sweetly kissed him. "What do you feel, Alessandro?"

He pulled his head back and devoured her with his eyes. "I love you, Julie." Her heart stopped beating and she thought she'd die. His smile was tender, *"Te amo, Giulietta. Veramente, Te voglio bene, Carissima."* So much better in Italian, she thought, and then she ceased to think at all.

✦ ✦ ✦

It was worse than he could ever have imagined. First, his mother's air of betrayed martyrdom in the kitchen when he woke up; then the whispers on the street when he went to get the bread. "What happened?" Chiara's eyes were round with apprehension. He saw Zara stop what she was doing and cock her head toward him, listening hard. His face showed his misery. He pulled Chiara away from the counter and into the alcove at the back.

"I'm in big trouble."

"What is it?" She bit her lip in concern.

"It's supposed to be a secret, but I think I have to tell you." He gripped her shoulders and quickly tried to explain what had happened and how everything had become unraveled. Her brown eyes got bigger and bigger as she listened. "So I need you to help me, Chiara."

"What do you want me to do?" He smiled tenderly at her. Thirteen years old and no questions or recriminations. What a girl!

"You have to find Massimo. I don't know where he could *be*! Tell him everything and tell him to come to Otto's house right away. He can think up some reason." He shook her tiny shoulders. "I'm scared, Chiara. I'm out of my depth here. I'm really afraid of Otto. I think he's the murderer, but we could be wrong. And even if he's *not* the murderer, he's going to hurt me bad." She bit at her bottom lip and looked up at him, her heart in her eyes.

"Don't worry, Anton. I'll help you. No matter what." She stood on tiptoe and quickly, like a butterfly touching his face, she kissed him on the cheek.

His mouth dropped open and they clung to one another. He bent his head, sliding his hands to the sides of her neck. He could feel the tiny beat of her pulse under his thumbs and it enflamed him with the first taste of real love. "Ah, Chiara." He kissed her open mouth gently. "You are just wonderful."

They could hear Zara's footsteps coming around the corner and they sprang apart. She saw the two of them with scarlet faces. "Here's your bread," she said, handing him a sack.

"Thank you, Zara," he mumbled, and in a flash, he was gone. Zara watched him run down the street and with a grin on her face, motioned to Chiara to get back to work.

✦✦✦

At the first light of morning, Massimo kicked Umberto Talerico out of bed. Groaning and moaning, his hangover the most massive he'd ever had, Umberto was prodded unmercifully by Massimo's big foot in its regulation boot until he finally stumbled along the road to help the village policeman change his flat tire. "Move your fat ass, Umberto, or I'll arrest you myself!" Massimo roared.

"For what?" Retching and shaking, Umberto cowered under Massimo's wrath.

"For beating your wife, for stealing her necklace, for getting drunk--and most of all, for wasting my *time*!" Massimo shoved him, stumbling, along the road.

✦✦✦

She awoke to his kiss. "Good morning, my beloved." He was inches from her face, his thick eyelashes spiked together and the love in his eyes shining clear. She wound her arms around his silky back and pulled his mouth to hers. "Oh, Alessandro. I love you so." He moved his mouth to her neck and nibbled at the tender spot just under her ear. She thought she'd die from happiness. She opened her eyes lazily, holding his tousled head closer to her, stroking it and rapturously rubbing her face against it. They'd managed to find their way into the guest bedroom, she noted, although she didn't quite remember how. She giggled and he bit her neck, playful as only new lovers can be.

Hmmmm, the pretty flowered sheet was in the way, wound around his torso. She reached down and pushed it aside and then captured him. "Alessandro?"

"*Carissima*," he moaned in delight. "I love you as life itself. There never was a woman like you, I swear. We will be together, you and I, *Carissima*, until eternity, making one another smile. Come, my darling. Tell me how much you love me." His hands were everywhere, doing everything and she was nearly drowned again.

"I love you, Alessandro," she gasped. "Ah, how I love you." And once again, they noticed nothing but themselves.

✦ ✦ ✦

Anton knocked gingerly on Otto's door. Nevermind that Otto had promised that he wouldn't use any violence; the man was a liar and a brute, not only a murderer. The first thing he did was cuff Anton on his ear. "Clean up this mess, you spawn of the Devil." He shoved Anton hard and the boy staggered to keep upright. "Here's a brush and some soap, you little rat." Otto threw a bucket at Anton, and stood, arms folded, watching as Anton went about trying to obey.

It was amusing at first to watch the little beggar work, and Otto took every opportunity to push, shove and kick Anton as often as he could. But some inner strength seemed to keep Anton calm and stoic. He kept his head down and worked as hard as he could, trying hard not to make Otto any angrier than he was already.

Pretty soon, Otto grew tired of standing and watching the boy. He sat down heavily at the newly cleaned table and drank a cup of coffee, his pig eyes never leaving Anton's face, taunting the boy as often as he could, making remarks about his dead, philandering father.

Anton kept himself sane by talking inside his brain. "Everything Otto is saying about my father was absolutely true. My father *was* a cheater and a philanderer." Only somehow, it was worse for Otto to talk about it. Anton gritted his teeth and tried to remember just why he'd gotten himself into this mess. To catch Otto. That's all he had to remember now. The pig would get his just desserts soon enough.

Only it was harder than Anton ever thought it would be.

Alessandro kissed her again, in sweaty, luxurious afterlust, then swatted her on her bottom as he got up to use the bathroom. She lay, face down, with one arm dangling off the bed, listening to the sounds of her beloved turning on the shower. She sighed, stretching luxuriously. She got up, naked and glowing, and stretched, unable to keep a silly grin from curving her mouth upward. He was wonderful. A strong and tender lover, better even than her wildest fantasies! Never had her body sung as it had done last night! And this morning, too, she giggled, her mood as bubbly as the champagne they'd drunk. Oh, Italy! You wonderful place, you!

She padded over to the window and peeked through the blinds. It was a *glorious* day. She danced a little happy dance and then, curious, began to poke around the room, humming a 50's song, "He's sure the boy I love, Wo Wo, Wo, he's sure the boy I love!" Would they live here? Would he want to come to the United States and meet her parents right away? It was a beautiful apartment. She opened the guest room door and glided into the salon, sinking her bare feet into the off-white carpeting, then tsk-tsking over the way they had strewn their clothes last night. Laughing, she picked up the white, backless dress and draped it over her arm. Should she try to find the kitchen and make them some coffee?

She drifted through the place, opening and closing doors and envisioning herself living here, in total bliss. She pushed his bedroom door open and stood, transfixed. So this was what his room looked like. Brown and blue muted colors. Strong furniture, mostly modern, with a few beautiful antique pieces. A blue velvet chair and a . . . *what was that?* She picked up the bright red nightgown on the bedspread, her face a puzzle. She fingered the frowsy feathers and her mouth opened a little. What? Was this some kind of a joke? She stubbed her toe on one of the high-heeled slippers lying tucked under the edge of the bed. She bent and picked one of them up, holding it by one finger, and then she noticed the letter lying on the pillow. Unable to help herself, she picked it up and read it.

"Carissimo Alessandro,

Oh, darling. I know you were so mad that I couldn't go to the opera with you. I just love it when you get mad and make all those big, manly noises. And, best of all, I love it when we make up and you drive me crazy with your desires. We will be so happy when we are married. I am wearing your ring, my love, and I will never take it off my finger. I can't wait to be your wife.

Your Carissima, Your Own Kitten,

Kendra

Kendra? Who the hell was Kendra?

✦ ✦ ✦

The boy was in the bathroom, cleaning the ancient tub, sink and toilet. It should keep him busy for the rest of the day after he came back from having lunch. "Hey, stupid. Go home and get your mother to give you some lunch." Otto looked at the expensive wristwatch he had on his arm, the one that he'd wrenched off his dead cousin's husband's wrist. "Be back in one hour. Don't let me catch you being one minute late!"

✦ ✦ ✦

Her mind was a white-hot blaze of fury. She picked up the red whore's nightgown, noticing now the faint smell of cloying perfume and some other faint odor. She held the nightgown distastefully in two fingers, noticing that the feather boa was molting over the floor. She stooped and picked up the two pom-pommed slippers and the letter and whirled back into the guest room. Alessandro was still showering, singling a merry tune at the top of his lungs and she could see the faint outline of his naked body as he soaped himself under the drumming water. She grabbed a glass from the sink and filled it to the brim with cold water. Bastard! *Bast*ard! She threw one of the slippers over the top of the shower curtain. He shouted in surprise, "What the hell!" And then she threw the nightgown over the top of the shower, right on top of his head.

He jerked the shower curtain open. "Wha . . . ?" Her temper flaring out of control, she threw the glass of cold water at his naked body. In some pinpoint of clarity, she was happy to see that the hot water had dissolved the cheap, red dye, and that Alessandro's head, shoulders and body were draped with rivulets of dripping red water and festooned with the remnants of the nightgown.

"*Kendra*!" She screamed, throwing the red pom-pommed shoe at his head. "*Kendra*! Your *carissima*, hey!" She spit out the word of endearment. "You gave her an en*gage*ment ring, you Italian louse, you!" His mouth gaped, but she could see some glimpse of startled embarrassment as he plucked at the red nightgown's wet drape. "You . . . You . . . Well, fuck you, Alessandro, you . . . you . . . ." She didn't mean to do it, but she started to cry. "I trusted you, you bastard," she hissed through her sobs. "I gave you my heart!"

He stood there, his mouth open, unable to comprehend what was happening. "Julie! Julie, please . . . wha . . . ," But she had slammed the bathroom door and by the time he grabbed a towel and tried to grab her, she was gone.

CHAPTER THIRTEEN

"So, Giorgio, what's new?" The second shift manager of *Stella Auto Noleggio,* breezed into the office, a salami sandwich and a thermos of coffee tucked under his arm.

"You just missed a lulu?"

"Yeah?"

"Yeah. A real bimba. Red hair, wearing her working clothes from last night's revelries." Giorgio lit up his last cigarette before he went home to get some sleep. "She came in about an hour ago to rent a car for the day."

"A real *putana?*"

"What else?" He shrugged. "Who else would be wearing silver shoes and a long white dress that went all the way down to her ass in back at this time of the morning?"

✦ ✦ ✦

She'd managed to drive the car out of Milano and onto the *autostrada,* but as soon as she got to the first rest stop, she pulled over. She just couldn't manage to drive any more. She huddled in the car with the heater turned up to full blast, shaking and shivering, bawling her head off, with her heart broken in tiny pieces.

She must have cried herself to sleep. She awoke with a neck wrenching jerk, wildly disoriented, not quite knowing where she was for a moment. She looked at the clock in the car. Nearly two! She must have slept for hours! She checked herself in the mirror and shuddered. She looked like the cat's dinner from last week. Her eyes were red and puffy and her hair lay in matted clumps on her head. She looked down at herself and snorted. She couldn't even go into the rest stop and get a cup of coffee dressed like this! They'd think she was some streetwalker!

She sighed, weary to the bone. She was just like some streetwalker, wasn't she? Throwing herself at Alessandro, giving herself to him and thinking that he felt the same way, when all the time he had this Kendra woman, and was even engaged to marry her. "I'm such a fool," she started to cry again. "I was easy, Alessandro, wasn't I? The stupid *Americana*. I fell for your lies, hook, line and sinker." She felt sick and rolled down the window to get some fresh air on her face before she started the car for the long journey back to Malafortuna.

✦ ✦ ✦

Where the hell had she *gone* to? He'd searched all over the building and ridden slowly around the local streets. He ought to be able to find her, after all, how many women were running hysterically around Milano wearing a white, backless evening gown?

He headed for Malafortuna. Where else could she be?

As he drove, he planned how he would get even with Kendra. Killing her was too good for her. It would have to be something much, much worse. Cutting off all her hair or breaking her nose. Finding a picture of what she looked like before she had all her plastic surgery! *Merde*! He pounded the steering wheel. How the hell had this whole thing happened?

He drove like a demon, making the red Ferrari go faster than it ever had gone. He sped by the rest stop, never noticing the green rented car parked at the far end of the parking lot. The one with the girl in the white dress who was fast sleep with tear marks staining her cheeks.

He tore into Marina's yard, the tires spitting up grass and flowers and one yellow shrub.

"Where is she?" He yelled at his sister.

"Who?"

And he told her. She sat down, stunned at the viciousness of this woman, Kendra's lies.

"Oh, Sweet Virgin Mary! Poor Julie!"

"Poor Julie?" For a moment he raged and then, slowly he slumped down at the table.

"Yes." He said quietly. "I broke her heart, I think. And if I don't get her to listen to me, I'll break my own." He gave Marina a hunted look from under his thick brows. "I love her, Marina. Honestly and truly, and I will kill Kendra if I can't somehow explain this mess to Julie."

"Is there anything I can do?" He shook his head, sick to his soul.

Marina got him a glass of wine. "This Kendra, does she mean anything to you?"

"She's just some bit of a model that I see once in a while." Marina had a momentary sense of sympathy for Kendra. Alessandro was a handsome man. "She means nothing at all to me."

"And Julie?" She looked hard at her brother's misery.

"I want to marry Julie," he said flatly. He looked so sad. Some little imp in her mind prodded her. He'd gotten himself in some mess, hadn't he?

"I'm sorry, Alessandro. You'd better find her soon and explain everything to her." He looked bleakly at her. "Maybe if you throw yourself at her feet, she'll listen." And to get his mind off his problems and remind him that the rest of the world didn't always go smoothly, she told him a little of her own troubles, " We've had a little bit of excitement here, too." Alessandro barely looked at her. "Maybe not as bad as what you're going through, but to me, it's very serious. I don't know what to do about Anton." She sat back down and cradled her head in her hands. Alessandro heard her voice and then he knew that she was crying.

"What's wrong?"

She shook her head dolefully and then told him what Anton had done

Alessandro swore softly under his breath. "I'd have sworn that the kid was all over that kind of behavior. I'd have sworn that he'd never do anything like that again." He went over to his sister and put his arms around her. "I've been a poor uncle to him, and a poor brother to you. Julie was right. I am a selfish son-of-a-bitch." Marina patted his hand and shook her head.

"You've been busy with your own life, Alessandro. You can't blame yourself for Anton's behavior."

"No, but I can give the boy a good talking to when I see him. Maybe I can knock a little sense into his head." His face was miserable. "And give him some love and happiness while I'm at it."

Marina's dry laugh echoed through the kitchen. "Well, here's your chance. I see him coming down the street, with his lip hanging down as far as his shoes. He's coming home for lunch."

"You get out of here. Leave him alone with me for lunch. I'll scare the daylights out of him and I promise you he'll never act like this again." Alessandro sat at the kitchen table

"Buon giorno, Anton. "

"Zio Alessandro!"

"Sit down, my boy." Alessandro's voice was steel. "I understand that you've been making your mother cry again!"

"No! Zio! You don't understand!"

Alessandro's nerves were raw. Perhaps, at another time, he'd be more patient with his nephew. Perhaps he'd be more discerning, and have discovered the root of the problem as to why Anton had misbehaved. But not today. Today, he ripped Anton a new rectum. He ranted and raved and swore and threatened and finally, Anton began to cry.

"You know nothing, Zio!" The boy was brave, Alessandro noted.

"I know that you've made your mother sad and disgraced yourself in the village."

"And if you and Renzo had been caught so many years ago, putting the goat in the church, you, too, would have disgraced the village and made your mother cry." Alessandro stopped dead in his tracks. What was the boy saying? "But, no! You're the great Alessandro Alessi! You never do anything wrong! You don't understand anything!" Alessandro tried to cling to his expression of disgust. "You think because you're the big boss that you know everything! Well, you don't!" And Anton turned and ran out of the house, wiping his eyes on the sleeve of his shirt.

Alessandro looked at his departing back thoughtfully. If his nephew only knew what a mess he'd just made of his own life. The kid was right. He didn't know anything! He just ruined the love of the most important person ever to come into his life!

Anton went back to Otto's house slowly, scuffing his feet. Was there no one who understood what he was doing? No one who could realize the sacrifice he was making to catch this criminal! Where the heck was Massimo?

✦✦✦

High up, just over the top of the mountain, Massimo finally got his car to get going again. Cursing, he'd driven Umberto all the way back home again.

"Are you going to arrest me?" Umberto asked fearfully. In answer, Massimo kicked him out of the car.

Only a few more miles and he'd be over the crest of the hill. Then, thank The Blessed Mother, he'd be able to use the cell phone and get in touch with civilization again. He wondered if Marina had missed him at all. His mother might have been disconcerted to know that he hadn't thought of *her* at all. Nonna would have been delighted that he hadn't.

✦ ✦ ✦

Otto's laugh rumbled deep in his chest as he watched Anton bent over the toilet. "Hey! *Ragazzo stupido*! I'm going to go out for fifteen minutes." Anton nodded his head, but kept scrubbing. "Don't dare go into my bedroom or touch any of my private things." Anton nodded, letting an expression of fear cross his face. "Don't even *think* of stopping your work." Anton nodded again. "Or else, I'll kick your ass when I get back. I want that toilet bowl *gleaming*!" Otto shook his fist as a warning to Anton. Satisfied that he had frightened the boy enough, he grunted and left the house, walking towards the *taverna* for a shot of grappa to throw down his double chinned throat.

Anton waited until Otto's footsteps receded, then, leapt over the tub and stood, stock still, in the middle of the kitchen, trying hard to think where Otto might leave the spoils of his murders. The bedroom seemed the most likely place, especially as Otto had warned him to keep out of it. Actually, it was quite easy to find the four suitcases stuffed under the stale smelling, unmade bed.

He pulled one of them out. There was a brass tag hanging from the handle. He turned it over.

ANNABETH STANLEY
23 EVERGREEN ROAD, PORT CHESTER, NY 11230

Dry mouthed, he clicked the two latches on the side. The suitcase top lifted, revealing neat piles of clothes. He slid his hand underneath and felt thick wads of paper, and then a small box. He knelt down, pulled out the box and opened it. Inside was a pile of jewelry, rings, bracelets and a thick gold necklace. A fragrance, sweet and a little cloying, wafted out of the suitcase. Anton swallowed thickly.

A noise made him turn. "And what did you find, you curious little boy?" Otto stood, only a foot or so away and before Anton could cry out, Otto had smashed his fist into Anton's face.

❖❖❖

The telephone rang. Alessandro grabbed it up, "Julie?"

A loud, male voice started to laugh. "Nah, this is Julie's brother, Moe. Who's this?"

"Moe!" Alessandro held on to the receiver as if his life depended upon it. "This is Alessandro Alessi."

"Hey, Al. How the hell are you? I hear you and my sister are gettin' along real well. Glad to talk to you. I presume we'll me meeting soon." Moe's cheerful voice went on and on.

"Moe, please. Actually, things are not so good . . . " Alessandro was shaking.

"What's the matter, Al? What's wrong?"

"Oh, Moe," Alessandro's voice was pitiful. "I've been such a stupid man. I've made such a mess. I badly need some help."

The men talked for a half-hour. "And don't forget . . . A ring, a big one." Moe wound up his advice. "No! Wait! *Not* a big one, Al. No." Alessandro listened humbly. "No. Wait, let me think . . . A big ring, *I* should give to Blanche, and not a moment later than after this telephone call. You've made me realize that I've taken her too much for granted. Blanchie, she's a solid girl. Real, no frills. She *needs* a great big ring from me. And she deserves it today." Moe was doing some thinking himself. "But you and Julie. No. Not a big ring . . . ," He thought hard for a moment. "You have a grandmother, Al?"

"A grandmother? Sure, sure. What are you getting at?"

"I got it, Al. Go talk with your grandmother. Here's what to say . . . ." Alessandro hung up the phone. Al? Well, OK. Al, it would be. He ran to his mother's house, just missing the telephone call from Massimo who was driving as fast as he could on the road towards Malafortuna.

❖❖❖

Chiara was getting worried. She'd made excuses to leave the bakery a dozen times and she'd walked up and down the village square, trying to see into the windows of Otto's house, getting more and more fearful that Anton seemed to have disappeared.

"What's wrong with you?" Zara finally asked her. She bit her lip and shook her head. She'd promised Anton not to say anything.

✦ ✦ ✦

"Nonna?" He opened the kitchen door. The table was full, with his mother, grandmother, Claudio Boccadoro, the *postino*, and Mayor Biasi's wife having mid-afternoon tea. They were only missing a brass band. Could a man never have any privacy at all in Malafortuna?

" '*Giorno,* Alessandro." His grandmother smiled fondly at him, noting that the President of one of Milano's largest corporations seemed pale today.

"Nonna," he said, and then stopped. Eight pair of eyes stared, waiting. "Um . . . ." He floundered, helpless. His mother's head was tipped to the side, watching him. Claudio Boccadora's flapping mouth was stilled for once. Nonna Caterina gave him an encouraging look. What did the boy want?

I'm a drowning man, he thought. I have no dignity left at all. None. However, I deserve it. If she'll only have me back, I'll never, *never*, be a pompous ass again. Never. He took a deep breath. "Nonna, please. I need your help," he said humbly, and then he told everyone in the room what he'd done and what he needed.

CHAPTER FOURTEEN

Chiara squirmed as she took Signora Delia's endless order. She was so worried that she gave out twenty thousand *lire* in extra change. "What is *wrong* with you?" Zara pinned her down. "You're acting like an imbecile. What's the matter? Come on, you can tell me. What is it?" Zara gathered her in a warm embrace. "Tell Zara, sweetheart."

"Oh, Zara. I'm getting so worried!" Chiara wrung her hands. "It's Anton. He . . . " And crying, she shifted her burden to the woman who had also been a mother to her.

Zara listened to the tumbled, incoherent tale. "Come on, let's find Massimo or Marina." She yelled for Teodora, and the three of them shut the bakery and ran out of the house. On the way to Marina's, Chiara told her mother everything that Anton had told her.

At Marina's house, they met Alessandro. "Tell him everything, " Teodora urged.

The telephone rang. It was Massimo. "Oh, *Dio*! No! He promised me he wouldn't do anything! Marina's going to kill me for encouraging him!"

"I'm heading over to Otto's to get the boy. I don't care about Otto. I just want to make sure that Anton is safe!" Julie and his problems were shoved aside. They'd find the time and place to mend their lives when Anton was away from Otto's household. "How far away form Malafortuna are you?"

"About an hour. I feel so stupid and helpless. Christ! Marina is going to be so mad at me!"

"Let's worry about our women later. I'm going right over to Otto's. God forbid if he really is the murderer! Call me again in ten minutes." Alessandro hung up and gathered the little group together for its mission to get Anton away from any danger.

♦♦♦

It seemed to take her forever to drive back to Malafortuna. The mountains loomed over her. How had she ever thought that they were beautiful? This awful road! She hated it! As a matter of fact, she hated everything in Italy! She couldn't wait to get to her room, pack all her things, and go home to Connecticut

The road snaked around sharp corners and then she found herself up at the lookout. She stopped for a moment, suddenly remembering Annabeth and Elgin. She brushed a tear out of her eye. She'd leave their avenging to those who knew how to get such things done. Why had she ever thought that she could figure out who murdered them? She couldn't even run her *own* life without falling over herself. She felt a huge stab of pity for the two butchered people. Hopefully, Massimo can do something about it all. She sniffed and blew her nose and started down the road again.

His face filled her mind. "Oh, Alessandro!" She wailed, as wretched as she'd ever been in her life. "Why did you make such a fool of me? Why?" She cried out loud, and her cries echoed off the precipices looking down on the valley. She was so miserable. She burst into tears, paying no attention to the road. The car caromed off the flimsy guardrail that protected the road from dropping off into a crevice. She tried to straighten out the wheel, but she couldn't see through her swollen eyes and the tears that fell like a waterfall. The car banged into the side of the mountain, then, as she twisted the wheel, almost ran off the road. She screamed then, calling Alessandro's name out loud, losing control. The car smashed into a pile of rocks, stopping suddenly, with one wheel dangling over the side of a three-hundred foot drop.

She sat, still, frightened to move, seeing only space in front of her through the windshield. The dust and dirt from the car's momentum settled, and the air was still.

Carefully, afraid that the car would topple over, she eased herself over to the passenger side. For one heart-stopping moment, the car slid forward, causing a shower of rocks and gravel to slide off the mountain. "Oh, God! Alessandro, please help me." She prayed. "Please, ohpleaseohplease!" And the car was still, rocking slightly.

She couldn't just sit here. The car was going to fall over. She bit her lip so hard that she cut it. Dear God, she bargained, Get me out of this. I don't want to die just yet. Please. I want Alessandro! Gingerly, she moved, inch by inch and then she slowly, easily, opened the passenger seat door, pushing it with her fingertips, trying to keep as much weight on the seat as she could.

The door swung open and another shower of stones slid down the mountain. She felt the car begin to slide. She pushed hard and threw herself out of the door, smashing onto the road in a tumbled, filthy heap. One shoe had caught into the doorjamb and she watched, her heart in her throat, as the car moved away from her, falling, falling . . . in a crumble of rocks and screeching noise, over the side of the mountain. She lay there, huddled in shock, listening to the crashes it made as it fell, until she heard the biggest crash of all, and then everything was still.

✦ ✦ ✦

"He's not here." Bruno Bastingliata told them. "He loaded up a bunch-a rubbish and drove his truck away about ten minutes ago." He pointed over to the road that led out of Malafortuna. Zara and Chiara ran into Otto's house to search for Anton.

"Was anyone with him?" Alessandro nearly shook Bruno's head off.

"Nope. He was all alone. What's da matter?"

"You didn't see Anton?" Bruno shook his head, no.

Chiara ran out of the house, dancing up and down in agony. "There's no one in the house!" She grabbed Alessandro's arm. "All the stuff is all thrown around!"

"What's goin' on?" Bruno asked again.

"Tell me just what you saw." Alessandro's voice was steel.

"He came outta da house with a bunch a suitcases. Then he went back in a brought out a big, long rug, all rolled up. He threw everything in his truck, an' he drove off." Bruno shrugged his heavy shoulders. "That's all I know."

Chiara's eyes were huge. "Anton! He's got Anton in the rug! He's going to *murder him!*" She grabbed Alessandro's arm and pulled him. "Come on!"

"Wait!" Alessandro pulled out his cell phone. Quickly, he contacted Massimo and related what had happened. There was only stunned silence as Massimo tried to comprehend.

"Which way did Otto go?" Massimo's voice was a croak of despair.

"Up there!" Bruno pointed to the road to Torriano.

✦ ✦ ✦

After a while, she got to her feet. There didn't seem much purpose in only one shoe, so she kicked it off and then stood in the middle of the road, wondering what she should do. She was nearer to Malafortuna than Torriano. She shrugged, almost in a daze, and began the long, long trek, especially barefoot and in a ripped and tattered long white backless dress, back to Malafortuna.

✦ ✦ ✦

"Massimo, you take the high pass road. That should bring you up past Malafortuna and get you up above Otto." He could hear Massimo's grunt of assurance. "I'll go over the goat track and try to get ahead of him just past the overlook."

"*The goat track*? You'll rip the guts out of your Ferrari!"

Alessandro then told him what the Ferrari could do to itself, should Ferraris ever be able to perform such things. "Keep in touch with me ever five minutes, *amico mio*. We'll get the bastard, one of us!"

He started to run to the Ferrari, but Chiara clung like a burr to his arm. "I'm going to go with you," she shouted.

"You can't, *Carissima*," he winced slightly at his use of the diminutive, "It's too dangerous."

"I don't care! I want to see that Anton is all right!"

"Chiara, I need you to go to Marina's house and wait for her. Tell her or tell Julie, whichever you see first, what's happening. Also call Renzo Nulla. Tell him everything. After all that, call the police station in Torriano. Explain as best you can what the situation is, and then get Julie to drive you and Marina up the mountain to meet us all. With luck, we should overtake Otto about ten kilometers on the Torriano side of the overlook. Murderer or no murderer, Otto's a dangerous man! Got it?" She nodded, reluctant. "Good girl. Have your mother and Zara get some blankets and some first aid supplies, just in case."

"Just in case what?" She was a perceptive child.

"Just in case." He slapped her gently on her bottom. "Now *go*!"

He leapt into the Ferrari and hoped he remembered how to get to the goat track. He hadn't even thought about the goat track for more than fifteen years. A treacherous, snaking road, used only by the most nimble of goats, it stretched over the top of the mountain, where no car could really be driven.

When they were boys, he and Renzo used to race one another, seeing who could run the fastest, up the mountain and then back down again. He prayed that it wouldn't be impossibly blocked and that he could get through it. If he could, he might just be able to double back along the regular road and meet Otto coming towards him. Please, *Dio,* let the boy be all right and safe from this monster, he prayed. Please. And then, if all went well, he thought he might strangle Otto with his own hands. Afterwards.

Before he got out of the village, he saw Marina walking home along the side of the road. He screeched to a stop. "Get in," he shouted to her, motioning with his hand. "Quick!"

"What's wrong?" He reached over and slammed the door, revved the engine and shot off, turning into the fields where he remembered the goat track started. "What is it!" She screamed in alarm, watching his demented face. Over the rumble of the sound that the wheels made as they started over the rocky track, he told her.

✦ ✦ ✦

She had no idea of how long she'd been walking. A lifetime? An hour? The diamond-hard stones on the road had already cut her feet cruelly and the pain was sharp and dull at the same time. It hurt so much that she almost forgot the pain in her heart, but not quite.

The noise that the truck was making as it labored up the hill penetrated the ache inside her head. Someone was coming. She stopped and stood still, waiting in the middle of the road. Whoever it was, they'd take her back to Malafortuna, and then she could bathe her feet and get away from this horrid place.

The truck rounded the corner and stopped dead ahead of her. She stumbled to the passenger door and pulled it open. "Thank good . . . . Oh! *Oh!*"

Otto's ham-fisted hand reached down and pulled her into the cab. She was so stunned, so tired, so shocked, that she didn't even think of protesting.

Otto's laugh filled the truck. He shook her by the back of her neck. "Look at what *I* got!" His hand pushed her, bruising her upper arm. "I got you both!" She didn't exactly know what he was talking about, but the hair on the back of her neck stood up in abject fear.

"Wha . . . what do you mean?" She managed to ask?

Laughing some more, he told her. Told her about the letter from Annabeth. "I didn't even know I had a stupid cousin in America. And damn his eyes, Zio..how could he leave *her* the property? It was mine . . . *mine*!" Through her terror, she almost felt sorry for Otto. And then she heard the rest of his story. How he realized that no one in the village would know that he'd gotten the letter. How he'd written back, urging Annabeth and Elgin to come to Italy. "Such stupid names! How easy it was to fool them!" How he lured his cousin and her husband to the lookout, how he'd sliced their necks, how he'd covered his tracks by taking every incriminating thing. Julie shuddered and groaned.

Otto laughed again and the sound cut through her soul. "I killed them as easy as I kill the chickens on the farm!" He banged on the steering wheel. "How could they think of taking what was mine? I was Zio's heir! It was *mine*! Everything was supposed to be left to me! *Me!*"

He turned in the seat, nearly letting the truck run off the road. "I was so angry! Shit! How could they just come and take everything away? I *had* to do something, no?"

Frozen, she nodded, trying to think, trying to get her mind working.

"The bitch thought that I'd be delighted to see her! 'Dear Cousin', she kept calling me in the letter! I spit on 'Dear Cousin'!" He spat out of the window. "I had to kill them. You understand, don't you? What else could I do?"

She shivered and knew that she was going to die.

They kept in touch by cell phones. Marina had to hold Alessandro's, as he needed both hands to maneuver the Ferrari around the stumps sticking out of the road, the deep pits, and the boulders. "Are you gonna make it?"

"Pray, Massimo, pray."

"Where are you, Massimo?"

"I'm driving as fast as possible, Marina. I'm nearly over the top of the pass."

"Be careful!"

And there was silence for a few moments. Massimo could hear dreadful scrapes and metallic sounds from the open receiver.

" 'Sandro? What's happening to your car?"

"He's denting it." Marina told him. "We just crashed over a big rock and I think the mirror on my side of the car fell off. This is a scary road."

"Marina.can you hear me?"

"I hear you, Massimo."

"I . . . I didn't mean for Anton to act alone like this." Massimo sounded miserable. "I honestly didn't know he'd go ahead by himself . . . ."

"I understand. Everything will be all right." Her voice was still and calm.

"Marina?"

"Yes?"

"I love you."

"What?"

"I've always loved you. Right from the time I was born, I think."

"Massimo, you're crazy!" Alessandro's mouth twitched, in spite of himself.

"No. No I'm not crazy, Marina. I simply love you. I wanted you to know."

"Massimo," her voice hissed through the air currents. "You don't know what you're saying."

"Yes I do. Marina, when we have Anton safe and Otto is in prison, will you marry me?"

"Massimo!"

"Please. I love you. I've always loved you. I've waited and waited and waited for you. There was never anyone else."

"Never anyone else! You've had half the women in Italy!" Marina's voice was a screech. Alessandro turned his laugh into a deep cough and tried to concentrate on holding the car on the road . . . Or the goat track, as it truly was.

"I've had lots of women. But they were nothing to me. I was only passing time, praying that somehow, we could be together as man and wife." Marina's mouth opened and shut soundlessly. She couldn't think of anything to say. "Marina?"

"I'm here."

"So will you marry me?"

"For God's sakes! Not now! We'll talk later."

"I want to know now. I promise you I'll be a good father to Anton. And Marina?"

"Hush, Massimo!"

"No, I want to say it all now. We can have more babies, can't we, Marina?"

"Massimo!"

"Tell me yes or no, Marina . . . . Alsessandro! *I see the truck!*"

"Where?" Alessandro yelled towards the vicinity of the receiver.

"Right at the top of the overlook! I can see the stuff in the back! The rug! Anton! Ah, Anton! I can see Anton's feet thrashing around! He's OK, Marina. Dear Sweet Lord, Marina. Anton's all right!" Massimo's voice was choking with tears. "I see him!"

"Can Otto see you?" Alessandro yelled.

There was a pause. "No, I don't think so. I'm up above and in back of him. I should be right above him in about ten kilometers. Maybe about six minutes more."

"Be careful, Massimo!" Marina yelled into the cell phone. "Can Anton see you?"

"'No. The rug is over most of his body. But I can see his legs kicking like mad. He's trying to get loose. What a boy!" He whooped with excitement. Then, "Sandro, where are you?" Massimo's voice was sharp.

"Almost at the end of the goat . . . umph! . . . track. I'll be out of here in two minutes or so. Will I be ahead of him?" There was a crash of metal as the Ferrari lost most of its left back fender.

"I think so, old friend. I think we've done it!" Massimo sounded almost jubilant. "Marina!"

"Yes!"

"Yes, you'll marry me or yes, you heard me?"

She had to laugh. "Massimo! Stop it! We're going over the top - Ah, sweet Mother Mary! "

Alessandro forced the Ferrari's hood over a hump of grass. The car lurched and almost stalled, then nearly teetered on its undercarriage. "Come on, you beauty," Alessandro urged it. "Come *on*!" And the car's engine snarled and it swarmed over the obstacle. In a moment, they had bounced onto the roadbed.

"*I see you! I see you*!" Massimo screamed. "You made it! You're a mile underneath him heading toward him."

"Thank you, *Dio del Mondo!* Thank you!" Alessandro's whoop nearly split Massimo's eardrum.

"What are you going to do?"

"I'm gonna ram his face down his throat!"

"*Marina*!" Massimo's voice pleaded.

"Blessed Mary! I'll marry you! I'll marry you!" The car roared around the corners, picking up speed. Alessandro's face was set in a snarl.

"Marina?"

"*What now?*"

"Do you love me?"

"*Gesu*! Massimo! I must, mustn't I!"

"Watch out! You're almost there!" Massimo screamed. His own car had snaked down the mountain pass and was almost parallel to Otto's truck, a little behind it and about twenty feet above. "I'm going to be right over him in a second!"

Otto's truck lurched around the corner and Julie tried hard to hold herself against the door. Her teeth were chattering with fear. Otto had killed Annabeth and Elgin. As soon as they got to the clearing near Torriano's outskirts, the one near the swamp, she knew he was going to kill her and Anton. There was no way that she could think to stop him. His wheezing laugh burst out again. "But before I kill you, little American girl, you and me, we are going to have a little playtime." His hot finger traced an ice-cold line down her back. She tried to open the door handle, but it was stuck tight.

"I'll do anything you want. Just let the boy go."

"You're joking, little girl. He saw everything."

"I promise you that he won't tell," she was babbling. "Please, I'll . . . I'll give you money. My father is a rich American. He'll give you anything you want." Otto laughed even harder. "Please. Please. I'll give you anything you want!"

"Yes, you will." He laughed even more. "You'll do just what I ask you to, won't you?"

"I will," she bobbed her head up and down, terrified. Terrified. "Please, please, let him go." He reached over again and pinched her thigh with his porcine hand. He gripped the flesh hard, and twisted, making her eyes sting with pain. Maddened, she grabbed his hand and bit him, as hard as she could.

"Agggggh!" He cried out. The truck swerved hard, bouncing against the side of the hill.

He tried to steer it back into line as they caromed around a corner. "What the Hell!" he yelled. Coming straight at him, at blinding speed, was the red Ferrari. Alessandro was standing on the gas pedal, screaming, as the two vehicles slammed into one another.

Massimo stepped hard on his brakes and was out of the car before it even came to a stop. He heard the rip and tear of metal and looked down to see the car and the truck smash together. Marina was thrown out of the Ferrari, landing on all fours in the middle of the road. Alessandro's head bashed against the padded dashboard. Julie was thrown against the windshield and her head cut a bloody hole through the glass. Otto was crushed behind the steering wheel, unhurt, just pinned for an instant, saved by the fat of his stomach.

He roared and pushed the wheel away from his belly, wrenched the door of the truck open. Marina, dazed, was shaking her head. Otto started towards her, a tire wrench in his hand, ready to smash her down. There was an unearthly sound from above as Massimo launched himself down, flying thirty feet from the roadbed above, through the air, landing on Otto's back. Otto fell with the impact and in an instant, Massimo had him pinned, in one of the special grips that he'd been taught in the police academy in Potenza. He pushed Otto's face into the road, mashing it down as much as he could, screaming curses at the top of his lungs.

"Here!" Marina kicked Otto's head. Dazed, he lay on the ground. Marina tore at her dress, ripping a strip of cloth so that Massimo could tie Otto's hands. Massimo jerked Otto's head down again and tied his hands. Then he spit at Otto. Marina kicked again ineffectually at Otto's head, her fury making her wild. When his fat body was trussed, she ran around top the back of the truck. The rug had slid almost to the end of the truck bed, and was drooping off. She ripped and clawed at it. Massimo was there, helping her, and they unrolled it. Anton lay in the middle of the rug, trussed up like one of Nonna's chickens, gagged and bound. His eyeball's were nearly popped out of his head as he writhed and twisted, trying to get free from his manacles. "Anton!" His mother grabbed him and pulled the gag off. "Thank Saint Agnes that you are all right!" She hugged him, noting his slowly blackening eye and the bruises to his face. But he was all right and alive. She kissed him once and then dropped him back on the rug and ran over to help her brother.

Massimo, seeing that Anton was alive, also ran over to the Ferrari. Alessandro's face was bloody and battered, but he was groaning and trying to extricate himself from the car. Marina hopped on one foot in her agitation as Massimo tried to get Alessandro out. "Here. Let me help you. Wait! *Wait!* You idiot! Let me cut you free. Anton is fine. Alive. All right. *Wait!*" Massimo shook him, and then carefully pulled the twisted metal until Alessandro could get out.

The two men embraced, standing together with their arms around each other and then Marina threw herself on both of them. "We did it!" They exulted. No one knew that Julie was bleeding all over the front of the truck.

The three ran around the truck, with Massimo stopping for a moment to kick Otto in the stomach. They cut the ropes from Anton and hugged him tightly. "The suitcases!" Anton pointed to the rest of the things in the back of the truck, "All the stuff is in there. Their clothes, their papers, their jewelry. All the proof we need!"

"Good man," Massimo clapped him on his back, nearly sending Anton sprawling. "You caught him!"

"*I* caught him? He caught me!" Anton began to giggle, nearly hysterical. "I thought I would be dead. I lay in the back of that damned truck, trussed up in that damned rug, and thought that I would die!" He pounded Massimo on his back. "*You* guys saved me." He looked around, for the first time, noting all the damages. "What happened anyway?"

"Don't swear like that, Anton. It's not nice." Marina shook her finger at him. Anton blinked. Mothers! "Massimo came over the mountain and Alessandro came through the mountain. They're heroes, both of them. They saved your life." Marina started to cry.

"Then why are you crying?" Her son asked.

"Because I'm so happy!" Marina howled. "And because Massimo and I are going to get married!"

"*Married?*" Anton was stunned for a moment. "Well, good!"

Alessandro shoved Otto to his feet. "You pig! You murderer! You'll hang high for killing those two people."

Otto's laugh made their flesh creep. "And you," he spat contemptuously at Alessandro's face, "Me? How about *you*? You've killed *her*!" He made a motion with his head, and for the first time, they saw Julie's hair, red with the redder stain of blood, sticking through the broken glass.

"*Julie!*" Alessandro's face was drained. He leapt up on top of the truck and tenderly touched her head. "*Julie!*"

"Is she . . . ?" Marina's hand crept to her mouth and Anton moaned with fear.

She'd thought she was dead. She could hear everything, but, for some strange reason, she couldn't move at all. She tried to cry out. "Alessandro!" but it only came out as a faint whisper. "Alessandro!"

"Don't move, darling. Don't move a hair." He gently started to pick at the shards around her bloody face. She groaned pitifully. "Please, Julie. Stay still. Let me . . . ." He pulled each piece away, carefully, all the time talking to her, telling her how much he loved her. "I love you, Julie. I loved you from the moment I saw you, dancing out under the stars in the piazza.

Shhhhh, darling. Let me help you. I'm such and idiot, Julie. I hurt you and I know I'm not fit to sit at your feet, but I love you, love you, love you. " She made some inarticulate noise. "I know, *Carissima,* and you're my only *Carissima.* She was only a girl that I went out with. *Nessuno*, nobody. She was trying to make you mad at me. I never gave her any ring. I never asked anyone to marry me, except for Renata, of course." Now he was babbling, trying to tell her everything while her head was still imprisoned. In spite of the glass cutting into her neck, Julie smiled. He *did* love her. "And you know about Renata already, don't you? Ah, Julie. I love you so." She twisted her head gingerly, nearly freed. "And we are going to be married, right away, darling. And I will come to the United States and live with you, if that's what you want. I'll work on your father's garbage trucks." He could hear Marina and Massimo snickering, now that they knew that Julie was alive and well. Moderately well, anyway. Alessandro glared at them and continued his monolog. "But I hope you'll want to stay here in Malafortuna. And I'll leave the business. I think it would be a good idea if I started a school here. At the old monastery, you remember, Julie? The old place where we had our picnic?" She tried to say something, but her throat didn't seem to work. He saw something in her eyes and hope blazed like a beacon. "Ah, Julie, Julie. You do love me!"

She made some croak and he kept on talking, "The school, Julie. It will be wonderful. " He couldn't seem to stop talking. Telling her everything. Everything. "For boys like Anton who want to learn about automobile engines and how they work. What do you think, *Carissima?* And you can stay home and we'll have babies and you can cook. Whatever you want, my love. Julie? Julie, will you marry me?"

He put his hands on either side of her head and freed her, holding her and protecting her neck from the jagged edges. "See? Here. I have a ring for you. Here." He twisted the narrow, worn band of gold from his little finger. "It's Nonna Caterina's ring. It's for you, darling. Will you marry me?" He hadn't listened to Massimo woo Marina for nothing. "Please, Julie, is it yes, or no?" He sat back on his heels and watched her face anxiously.

Her eyes were still glazed and there was a buzzing in her head. He'd crashed his Ferrari and he didn't seem to care at all. He'd done it to save Anton. She loved him so. She peered at Alessandro's face. "Alessandro?" She whispered. He had his Nonna's ring for her! No man would dare mess around with his Nonna's ring. He *did* truly love her!

"Will you marry me, darling?" She shook her head and reached up, rubbing at the huge bump. She groaned as she touched it gingerly. Alessandro's beloved face swam into her vision.

"Alessandro? Did you ask me to marry you?"

"Yes I did."

She grinned at him. It hurt like hell, but she grinned anyway. "Did I say yes yet?"

"Yet? Yet?" His face was incandescent. "Oh, Julie!" And he gathered her tenderly in his arms. Otto spat on the ground.

There was a roar of engines and three police cars came around the bend, skidding on their brakes, narrowly missing the pile up in the middle of the road. Inspector Nargi jumped out of the first car, "What's happening here? Who is in command?"

"Oh, I am, Chief," Massimo draped his arms around Marina. "I'm definitely in charge here."

CHAPTER FIFTEEN

It took more than an hour to straighten everything out. Everyone was talking at once, everyone wanted to tell their story. They sat on the ground in a circle, Massimo and Marina and Anton with Julie slumped against Alessandro's shoulder. No one paid the slightest attention to Chief Nargi and his men as he barked out orders and fingerprinted everything in sight. No one even looked at Otto.

Another car was coming along the mountain. Renzo was driving, with Chiara, Teodora and Zara hanging on for dear life. Massimo jumped up and waved ecstatically at his brother.

"Is everyone all right?" Renzo leaped out of the car.

"Marina is going to be my wife!" Massimo yelled at him.

"What!"

"My wife!" Massimo pounded Renzo's back, thumping him and shaking his hand up and down. Everyone began to talk at once again.

Chiara slid over to Anton. "Are you alive?" Her dark eyes were impish.

Anton grinned at her and then, in front of his mother, her mother and everyone, kissed her sweetly on her open mouth. Zio Alessandro winked at him, and Massimo punched him lightly on the shoulder.

"Let's all go home," Julie managed to whisper. "Let's all go back to Malafortuna."

✦ ✦ ✦

Massimo Nulla was given a medal for his heroic capture of Otto Zampone. His wife and adopted son stood proudly with him on the platform while the *Direttore di Polizia* put the red, white and green ribbon around his neck. Chief Nargi stood behind several others on the podium, a sour expression on his face.

Massimo's medal came with a promotion and an increase in salary. In addition, a year later he was given a government automobile to use while on official business. One of the first such official business trips was to bring his new daughter, Graziella, home from the hospital.

❖ ❖ ❖

Julie and Alessandro were married in a small ceremony in Greenwich, Connecticut, one week before Moe and Blanche's huge wedding. Alessandro's gift to Julie was to charter part of an Alitalia airplane. A small contingent of people from Malafortuna; Sofia and Nonna Caterina, Renzo and Carmella, Signora Nulla and Nonna Graziella, Zio Nina and Zio Nunzio, Teodora, Zara and Chiara, Marina, Massimo, and of course, Anton, came to Greenwich to attend both weddings and to go to New York City to see the Rockettes perform at radio City Music Hall.

After Moe and Blanche's wedding, the bride and groom drove away in a brand new garbage truck.

❖ ❖ ❖

The Alessi School at Malafortuna became famous, graduating topnotch mechanical engineers and automobile designers. Anton Corbone Nulla (he took his stepfather's name legally) was their first graduate.

❖ ❖ ❖

And Julie's cookbook became an international best seller. She really didn't care how many copies it sold. She and Alessandro were too busy raising a family of five boys and three girls, easily beating out Renzo and Carmella.

❖ ❖ ❖

Three weeks after Julie and Alessandro's wedding, Carmella Nulla gave birth to a baby girl. They named her Julie Nulla. Julie was elated. "I told you it would be a girl!" she crowed. "And I'm so proud. I never had anyone name a baby after me before!"

"Don't you ever tell her," Carmella made Renzo promise, "that the baby was named after Julie Andrews." Renzo nuzzled the baby's soft, downy hair and wondered at the way of women. He kissed his wife's rounded shoulder and promised that he'd never breathe it to a soul.

Also written by J. Tracksler

The Botticelli Journey

Una Furtiva Lagrima/Un Di Felice

Cherubini

The Ice Floe

Printed in the United States
1269400005B/80